# The Real Maisy

# The Real Maisy

Nicky J. Mason

Copyright © 2024 Nicky J. Mason

The moral right of the author has been asserted.

Apart from any fair dealing for the purposes of research or private study, or criticism or review, as permitted under the Copyright, Designs and Patents Act 1988, this publication may only be reproduced, stored or transmitted, in any form or by any means, with the prior permission in writing of the publishers, or in the case of reprographic reproduction in accordance with the terms of licences issued by the Copyright Licensing Agency. Enquiries concerning reproduction outside those terms should be sent to the publishers.

This is a work of fiction. Names, characters, businesses, places, events and incidents are either the products of the author's imagination or used in a fictitious manner. Any resemblance to actual persons, living or dead, or actual events is purely coincidental.

Troubador Publishing Ltd
Unit E2 Airfield Business Park,
Harrison Road, Market Harborough,
Leicestershire. LE16 7UL
Tel: 0116 2792299
Email: books@troubador.co.uk
Web: www.troubador.co.uk

ISBN 978-1-80514-547-9

British Library Cataloguing in Publication Data.
A catalogue record for this book is available from the British Library.

Printed and bound in Great Britain by 4edge Limited
Typeset in 11pt Minion Pro by Troubador Publishing Ltd, Leicester, UK

"It is not our differences that divide us. It is our inability to recognise, accept and celebrate those differences."
**– Aurdre Lurde**

# One

Maisy bit her lip to stop the tears from coming. She was being fired, again? She'd only taken a few days off in the six weeks of working there. And those days were emergencies. Like when Roxy got dumped by that cringy photographer who went round smelling everything. Or the time she'd got so wasted that she couldn't even get up from the sofa because her head was spinning so fast. The day prior to the firing, she'd been unable to find parking. How was it her fault if they didn't have parking onsite?

"You're firing me because I couldn't find parking?" she demanded.

"Calm down, Maisy," he said in his usual nasal-sounding voice. "I understand you must be upset, but this is not just about today. In the six weeks you have been with us, you've had…" he peered at the computer screen, "seven occasions off."

"It is not seven occasions," she scoffed.

She stared at his yellow, uneven teeth. The front two lapped each other, and she wondered if they were difficult to brush. If it were her, she'd probably get Invisalign, or have had them replaced or something. *Dentists can do wonders these days.*

*Wait, what was he saying?* She caught the tail end of it.

"…then there was an occasion when you said you'd 'had an emergency,'" he air quoted, "and would be in by twelve. But you never came in. That was never explained, either."

She remembered that – she hadn't been able to get a salon appointment after work. She'd had no choice. She'd told them she'd be in by lunchtime. She had genuinely tried, too. But by then, her friends were already in the pub. What was she supposed to do? She glanced around the office, peering through the Perspex screen towards the other eight members of staff seated at their desks. Drinking coffee, chatting, and laughing as they tapped away at their computers. Would she ever fit in somewhere like that? "And what about Jasmine?" she asked, suddenly remembering. His eyebrows shot up and he stared at her, unblinking.

*Had he forgotten already?* "She was off for five days in a row last week, and you didn't say a word to her, did you?" she reminded him.

A funny noise came from his throat, as though he had a bit of apple lodged in it. "Maisy!" He looked around, as though worried someone would hear. "Her mother died!" he whispered between clenched teeth.

She narrowed her eyes at him. "Look, I have done some amazing work in this place. I spent hours on that last campaign, and it pretty much went viral."

"Pretty much. And yes, when you're here, you're a good worker. But you can be a little… hmm, unpredictable. You don't pay attention to details, and let's face it, we can't rely on you being here, can we?"

"What are you on about? I'm always here!" she declared.

He grimaced. "Except when you're not."

She should have been due a promotion for all the email campaigns she'd completed in the past week. And on Thursday, she'd come in half an hour early, but he hadn't remembered that, had he? What was he thinking? Maisy looked over at him through her Russian-style lashes. But he was looking at his computer screen now. Probably going through new applicants as she stood there. She'd blown it.

"Well, that's rude."

"Sorry. Anyway, good luck with the future." He seemed distracted. He stood up, ran a hand around the waist of his trousers, making sure his shirt was fully tucked. He used his other hand to balance himself on the table. "You'll be okay seeing yourself out, won't you?"

She glanced at her watch and tapped her heels against the floor. It was 6pm on Friday. *What would Ameera be doing right now?*

"Fine," she huffed.

She'd only got the job in the first place because her parents had been complaining about her hanging around the house and leaving a mess. Even though she was sure she cleaned the place more than they seemed to. And it wasn't like she hadn't tried in the past. She'd recently started up her own marketing company. It had gone bust within a few weeks, but she'd learnt loads from it. She figured if she got some experience under her belt, then maybe she could give it another try. But maybe marketing wasn't for her after all. People on Instagram and TikTok made it look fun, but it wasn't. She spent most of her time sat in a boring office, crunching numbers, and then she was expected to 'get creative' after they'd killed her soul with facts and figures.

Michael leaned over, putting out his hand to shake hers. "Best of luck for the future, anyway. I'm sure you'll find something more…" He hesitated. "Suited to your needs."

Maisy nodded, feeling the familiar tightening that gripped her lungs and clouded her brain. She smiled, pulled on her jacket.

"You're just lucky I'm not the type to take revenge."

"I beg your pardon? Was that a threat, Maisy?"

"No, I've got better things to do with my time," she said, sweeping from the office. She burst out of the door, like someone submerged in water coming up for air, then she leant against the reception wall, placed a manicured hand on her diaphragm and inhaled deeply. She'd been practising a technique called Buteyko specifically for moments like this. Once her breathing and self-affirmations were complete, she held her head up high and walked out of the doors past the huge lit up sign that read 'Montell's Marketing'.

She crossed the car park, planning ways of getting her revenge on Michael Montell. She imagined herself sending out a fake marketing campaign offering Michael's 'services' to all of the office. She stepped up the curb. *What is the saying? The best revenge is to succeed. Isn't that what people always said?* She sniggered to herself. Only the week prior, she'd been watching YouTube videos about realtors in America selling mega-expensive houses. It had inspired her to open her own estate agency, only for businesses. Renting and selling offices, factories, and warehouses. It was a niche. She could make it work. *And there is a lot of money to be made in property, isn't there? I'll soon be making way more money than Montell's. I'd look good with my picture on the front page of... what is it again?* Vice magazine? *The one where all the success stories go, about entrepreneurial badass women.*

She stepped over the road, a happy bounce in her step. *I am a badass woman*, she mused. *It just hasn't happened for me yet. I just need to find my USP.* She'd hated college. She'd tried being a sports masseuse, but it gave her backache. Plus, she hadn't enjoyed the hairy backs. She shuddered at the memory. Estate agency was where it was at. She always knew she was meant to be her own boss. There was a word stuck in her head; *prolific*, prolific what did that mean?

She dodged a couple of slow, elderly people meandering along the path, stopped to pet a golden retriever, and hopped out of the way of middle-aged shoppers and everyday office workers. As she passed the city courts a woman with glowing skin, dressed in a Ralph Lauren suit (the navy one with the notched lapel), some glossy black heels and a sleek black hairstyle stood talking to a younger girl. The girl was dressed in old-looking black trousers with small rips in them and wore a white creased blouse, sporting red blotches around her eyes.

"It's okay," soothed the suited woman as she squatted down to meet the girl's eye level. Maisy didn't miss the flash of red on the base of her slick black heels. "You did really well today." Her voice was warm like honey. *Was the suited woman a solicitor encouraging her client?* She decided it was possible; either way, the woman was elegant and offering solidarity to a young woman. She only looked in her twenties herself, possibly even younger than Maisy.

Maisy felt her mood flattening. She was twenty-five with no career, no man and she couldn't even help herself, let alone someone else. In addition to that, she was still living in her parents' house, overlooking what was now a brand-new housing site, under the watchful eye of her parents' home cameras. Things needed to improve. Quick.

She needed to talk to her friend. She slid her phone from her bag.

"Ameera?" she cried. "I got fired!" She paused and dodged to the left, before she got bashed into by a group of boys in matching black uniforms. One was walking backwards, another at the side dived into the other, snorting with laughter.

She straightened and stepped up her pace. It was beginning to rain, and the streets were darkening. "Okay, I'm just getting the car and I'll be over. Then I need to get home and have an early night. Seriously." She laughed into the phone. "Tomorrow I'm going to decide on my new future company, B2B Estates." She moved the phone away from her ear as her friend's screams of laughter, almost pierced her eardrums. "You'll see. Things are about to change for the better."

# Two

Finally, the landing light turned on. Relief eased the weight from her chest.

Maisy had been banging on the door for what seemed like forever. She'd called her mum, dad and brother's mobiles over and over. No one had picked up and it was starting to get cold.

The patio doors slid open. Her mum was standing behind her dad, glaring at her.

"About time, it's freezing out here," she said, stepping inside.

Kathy flicked on the kettle. "We were asleep! It's 4am," she said, stretching her arms and yawning. She placed three mugs on the kitchen counter.

Robert locked the patio doors, then turned to face her. "What are you playing at Maisy?" he asked.

"I tried to call you. I lost my key."

"Again?" he barked. "We have work in a few hours; you can't keep waking us up like this."

She flicked her heels off and wobbled unsteadily. "Would you have preferred I freeze to death? My feet are killing me as well. Can't believe you left me out there so long."

"Where have you been?" Kathy asked, turning to lean against the counter.

"Ameera's," she said.

Her father was pacing, hands in his pyjama bottom pockets, belly hanging over the top. Her tiny mother was watching her curiously. Maisy could see the familiar look of disappointment on her face.

"And you got fired again?" Robert asked.

"Who told you that?"

"The police!"

"What police?"

"Maisy, I was fourteen when I started taking responsibility for my actions. Fourteen! And I was working for beans. And you? You're twenty-five and have every opportunity and yet have no potential, no self-respect, no proper education. You treat the people who do try to help you badly. We can't keep supporting you, this is our time to save for retirement, travel the world or do whatever the hell it is we want to do."

"Shouldn't have kids if that's what you wanted to do with your life."

"That's not the point! We've done our time."

"I am not saying…" She felt her bottom lip wobble as she spoke. He cut her off again.

"Enough!" he shouted.

"You don't understand…"

"No, I don't bloody well understand," he grimaced.

"Stop cutting me off!" she screamed at the top of her lungs. She felt a wave of nausea.

Kathy put a hand on her husband's shoulder. "Robert," she soothed in her usual quiet tone. "Calm down or you'll send your blood pressure through the roof."

Miles stumbled down the stairs, rubbing at his eyes. "What's all the noise about?" he groaned.

"Where did you go after you got fired?" Robert asked her.

"Ameera's! I just told you that once. Are you bloody deaf?"

"Was it her idea?"

"Was what her idea, getting fired?"

"Maisy, your mother was worried sick when the police came round. My god… she thought something had happened to you."

Maisy's eyes widened. "The police came here?"

"Yes, where do you think?"

Miles laughed. "Dumbass. Didn't think you could just do that to someone's car and get away with it, did you?"

"What are you talking about? I didn't do anything to anyone's car! I got an Uber back here," she blurted.

"Oh my god, Maisy, how drunk *are* you?"

"We only had a few Proseccos and some strawberry schnapps. But I didn't drive, I wouldn't do that."

"He said you threatened him, Maisy. Right before it happened," said Robert.

"What? Who?" she asked, confused.

"Michael! When you got fired you threatened him! Less than four hours later and his car is trashed and… he finds a shit on the roof."

"A shit on the roof of his car?" she screamed back in horror. "Who would do such a thing?"

"Are you telling me this wasn't your doing?" Robert asked.

Maisy's stomach whirled; warm saliva filled her mouth. She leant forward. "Wait…"

"No, Maisy, enough is enough, do you know…" Her mum's voice was cut off by the sound of splashing on the kitchen floor. A strong stench like vodka and pungent strawberries filled the air. The three of them turned to see Maisy looking back at them, her clothes and hair dripping in vomit. Maisy gasped at the scene around her. A screech escaped her mum's mouth.

\*\*\*

Robert slapped his balding head with the palm of his hand. Kathy scurried out of the room and Miles burst out laughing. Robert turned and stared at his son. "Think this is funny, Miles? You're twenty-four and your sister is twenty-five. We shouldn't be dealing with teenage rebellions any longer."

Miles eyes widened. "What did I do? It's her that's going around shitting on cars!" He gasped.

Maisy's head shot around. "Oh, piss off, all of you. I did not do that! I've never been anywhere near his house."

Kathy came in with a bucket full of disinfectant and snapped on a pair of rubber gloves.

"Do you, or do you not, know where Michael Montell lives Maisy?" Robert asked.

"That's beside the point. I never went to his house."

"So, you do know where he lives, yes?"

"Yes, he's on Juniper Road. But everyone at Montell's knows that. We've all googled-earthed his bloody mansion."

"So, you knew where he lived. What's to say you didn't get so drunk that you don't remember going there?"

Her mum was on her hands and knees, scrubbing at the carpet.

"Do I seem that drunk to you, Dad? If I was capable of remembering his address and knew how to get there, don't you think I would remember going?"

Her father shrugged in response.

"Dad, I didn't go near his property, and you know it! You're always looking for excuses to be nasty to me. I hate living in this house with you lot, you're fucking vile to me. Treating me like I'm some kind of criminal. You'd think, being my parents, you'd know me better."

"Maisy, that's literally what they told us you've done. And you're in this state. What do you want us to think?" he asked.

"Oh, Mais… This is a new low, even for you." Miles chuckled. He was loving every minute of it, she could tell.

"Don't be so fucking stupid, Miles. Of course I didn't do that," she protested.

She needed to get away from her family. How could they believe this utter rubbish people made up about her? They were her family; they were supposed to support her when things went wrong.

"You must have been hammered, Mais."

"She was! Look at the state of her. Maisy, if this sick stains you're paying to have the carpet cleaned. This isn't fair on your mother."

"You can all piss off. What kind of family kicks a girl when she's down? You're such arseholes."

Her mum sat up onto her legs, she rubbed below her

nose with the back of a rubber glove and sighed, blowing the fringe from her forehead. "Can you both please give her some space? You know this won't help." She turned to Maisy. "Maisy, please calm down and stop swearing."

"No! He's talking to Miles about me like he knows how it went. He knows nothing. That's not what happened. You want me to pay for your carpet to be cleaned? Fine. I will as soon as I get paid. I'm not denying that I puked everywhere, or even that I was drunk – because I was, and I did. But I would never have shit on someone's car roof. That's vile. And I can't believe my own family would think that of me."

She walked away from them, into the hallway and to the stairs. She wasn't part of this family. They were always judging her. At least when she was out with Ameera, she felt like she could be herself without being judged. She would never have shit on someone's car roof, no matter how drunk she'd been. Ameera would believe her.

*Why is Michael doing this to me?*

She started walking up the stairs. Her dad and Miles both followed her into the hallway.

"Maybe you should hear her out, Dad. She's had a 'shit' morning," Miles said, grunting with laughter.

Maisy stopped at the top of the stairs and leaned against the banister listening to them.

"Miles!" snapped Kathy.

He looked at her, laughing so hard he had tears streaming down his cheeks. "Sorry, Mum, but we all make mistakes when we're 'shitfaced'," he said, covering his face. "Ask Maisy," he cried, in barely audible chuckles. He dropped his head, and his shoulders shook up and down.

Maisy tilted her head, eyes narrowed. Their father looked like he was at bursting point. The veins in the side of his head were now fully shiny and ready to rupture. "Quite frankly, Miles, I'm sick of it," he snarled. "I've worked so hard to ensure that you kids had everything that I didn't growing up and look where it's got me."

"To be fair, Dad, you're doing alright. Perhaps what you didn't have is what gave you all of that gumption," Miles said, wiping away the tears that streamed down his cheeks.

Maisy looked at him and smirked. She could always count on her younger brother to say something completely inappropriate, taking the heat off her. He didn't do it on purpose, of course. He just had a mouth that didn't know when to stop.

"I am. Maybe you're right, because now I have two adult-kids who behave like toddlers."

Toddlers? He was the biggest child she knew! She couldn't keep quiet any longer. "Or…" she called down the stairs. "Perhaps it's because you say crap like that." She glared at him. "I mean, what kind of a father says that about his own kids. You're the one with the problem, not me. You're the most negative person I have ever met. It's no wonder both of your kids are miserable and co-dependent."

Miles eyes opened wide. "What's wrong with me?"

"Negative? You're constantly outraged about everything, Maisy."

"Because I'm in this toxic house. If you just left me alone, I'd be fine."

"But we wouldn't! You create mayhem and leave mess all over the house for your mum to clean up. Neither of you do any real graft and yet somehow spend money like it has no meaning."

"Why do I always get dragged into Maisy's mayhem? I work full time," spat Miles.

"Yeah, sitting at a computer! I remember when I took you out on the yard on work experience. You didn't have an ounce of common sense."

"Well, you try and do what I do then! I doubt you'd be any good at figuring out why someone's computer is bugging out," Miles said. Maisy felt like eye-rolling. Miles could make this argument go on forever, and the sick was starting to dry into her skin, making it tight and itchy.

Maisy looked down and rubbed at her skin on her bare arms, watching the flakes breaking off. She desperately needed to shower now.

"Dad? Are you okay?" she heard Miles ask. She turned towards them. Robert's face was bright red and screwed up, like he was in pain.

She felt something deep in her stomach that ached. She wished they'd stop with all the guilt trips and drama. They always turned everything around and made it about them so that she'd feel like shit, and she did. She wanted the feeling to go away, needed to distract herself.

"For god's sake! He is just being dramatic," she yelled. "Don't tell me – it's all my fault, I've made Dad ill now. Had to make it about you didn't you, Dad? Way to go, I'm the bad guy, yet again."

Robert attempted to lean on the console table beside him and missed, crouching down on the floor. Kathy ran over to him, a look of concern etched on her face.

"Shut the hell up, Maisy!" she barked, kneeling down

beside him. Maisy was taken back, her Mum never snapped at her like that. "Robert?" she gasped.

"I'm okay, I'm okay," he said, but his voice came out different. Like he'd been on the whiskey all night. "Just had a dizzy spell, that's all," he said, but it didn't sound like him. His speech slurred, like his tongue had doubled in size.

Maisy stood on the stairs, staring down at her family. Her father's lips were white, his eyes had a vacant look to them. Miles was rubbing the back of his neck, his face all screwed up.

Her mother looked desperate. "Put your arm around my neck," she demanded.

Robert stared up at her.

"Robert! Put your arm around my neck."

"Just hold on." He groaned, his arms clenched up, his face red.

Kathy's eyes widened. "You are not okay. Let's get you to the doctor. There's something not right." Her mum was speaking quick and breathlessly, crouched by him, fumbling with the phone in her hand, and visibly shaking.

As she dialled a number, she glanced up, her face screwed up in pain. Her eyes met Maisy's. Maisy felt the tears as they streamed down her cheeks.

*What the actual fuck just happened?*

# Three

After spending half an hour trying to find a parking space, Maisy approached the huge sliding doors of the hospital. Outside was a woman in a wheelchair, wrapped up in a dressing gown, sucking on a cigarette like her life depended on it. People rushed in and out or hung around outside chatting in groups, many with visible injuries, others she couldn't tell if they were patience or visitors. Someone sneezed and she physically jumped, wrapping her coat tight over her chest and tucking her nose into the collar. She could almost see the grubby germs floating around her face, being sucked into her nose or mouth. When she approached the door's, they zipped open. Maisy was stopped by an invisible force. She'd been arguing with herself all the way there. Her father probably didn't even want her there, he'd probably blame her and if she tried to get her point across, everyone would see her as mean. Because he was the patient.

Worse still, she might even blame herself if he looked sick or fragile.

She turned around to walk away, then stopped. She was being a fool. She was here, she should go in or he'd think she didn't care. But she couldn't. She spun on her heel and sucked in a deep breath, frozen to the spot. She looked around and could feel the stares of strangers. Just then her phone rang.

"Miss Fowler?"

"Yes," she answered, relieved by the distraction.

"You called about a loan?" The man on the other end sounded young and cheery, like salespeople often were, uncomfortably sprightly.

She took in a deep breath. "Ah yes, I did. I'm starting a business and I need a little kickstart."

"Well, that's certainly something we do. Is it a limited company you're needing funds for?"

"It will be," she replied, rocking back on her heels and chewing her bottom lip against the cold.

"And what's the company name?" he asked.

"B2B Estates, err, Limited."

"Thanks, could I just take names of the directors, any company investors, company secretary if you have one, the company address and the company registration number please?"

Suddenly she felt like a fraud. She coughed and quickly adjusted herself before giving him her parents address. "I don't have the other details yet. I'm sorry. It's not got any further than the planning stage, mainly due to funds."

"Ahh, I see. And do you have a business plan that includes financial forecasting and the intended target market."

"Oh absolutely," she lied.

"Okay, well, let's go from there then. Would you like to come and see us, Miss Fowler?"

"Yes, that would be great."

"Okay. I actually have a cancellation today at three."

She glanced at her watch; that gave her three hours. She could make that.

"I'll be there."

"Great, see you at three. And Miss Fowler?"

"Yes?"

"Don't forget your business plan and company house details."

"Of course," she replied with a gulp. *Business plan? Company registration? Shit.* She ran back to her car. She needed to write a business plan and she had about two hours to do it.

\*\*\*

The next day, she had made it to the first floor of the hospital before she turned around. The day after that she made it all the way to his room. She stood outside, listening as he spoke to the nurse. He didn't sound like her dad. He sounded muffled and slow. Maisy felt the bile rising in her throat. She turned around and walked away. She climbed back up the concrete steps of the car park, guilt and weakness weighing heavy on her shoulders.

6pm traffic was building; she drove slowly, a haze over her eyes. She went over a roundabout, stared at the standstill cars queuing ahead of her, then turned absently, tiredness wearing her down. She glanced at the road sign. Juniper Road.

*Juniper Road. Of course! It's the road Michael lives on.*

She took a tight turn to the left, squeezing past the car

in front and onto the side street. She started scanning the numbers. *What am I doing here? What will I do if I find the house?* All she knew was that she needed to understand what had happened the night someone vandalised his car.

She parked on the main road outside of number 165, got out and walked over to his house. A large, detached place with a gravelled drive. Juniper Road was the only street she knew of locally where every building had a pool, a granny-annexe, and a driveway big enough for five cars.

Walking up the drive, she felt like she was in a land of giants. *Why does anyone need a door that big?* To the right of the building, she spotted the edge of a car. She peered around further. The car was dented. She glanced around, then crept to the side of the house.

A red Audi Q7 sat looking new, aside from the dented door and roof. The window had two lines of mud smeared down it.

"Aha!"

Maisy swivelled on her heal, jumping at the sound. "Jesus Christ, Michael! You scared the shit out of me."

"Well, you weren't expecting me, were you." He leaned back on his heals, his bean-pole legs flexing backwards. "I got rid of your little parcel, if that's what you're looking for."

"Parcel? Jesus, no! Why would I be looking for that."

"Came for a second round then, maybe. Only now, I have cameras."

He nodded towards the roof of the house. Maisy followed his eyeline to two tiny cameras perched below the facias.

"I'm not here to cause trouble, Michael." She showed him the flats of her hands, as though in defeat. "I just wanted to know why you fired me. Then told the police that I vandalised your car. All in one day."

"We already discussed why I fired you, that conversation went on way too long. I thought that was clear."

"And did your car really get vandalised?"

"Of course it did! Less than four hours after I fired you. And you have to admit, you can be a little, hmm, unpredictable."

"I thought you knew me better than that. I would never do something like this! It's not my style."

"Who else would do it?" His voice was rising. "Who else would come onto my property, smash up my car, and defecate on it. What would you think, in my position?"

She put a hand to her chest, taken back. "Well, I wouldn't just pick someone at random to blame." Her lip wobbled.

His jaw ticked. "I fired you!"

"That doesn't make me guilty!"

"I think it's time you left. If the police found out you were here – at my house now – you'd be in even more trouble."

She could feel anger bubbling low in her belly. She gulped it down, attempting to remain calm.

"They will see it wasn't me. I didn't do it, Michael. I was at my friend's house all night."

"Then you've got nothing to worry about, have you?"

"No, but I want to know who did do it too. Because you're giving me a bad name. I think that's defamation or something, maybe I should be calling the police on you," she said, pointing a finger in his face. "How will I find another job with this lingering over my head?" His Adam's apple bobbed. "Even though I've never been anything but gracious towards you," Maisy continued.

His eyes searched the front door, his jaw still tight. "I'm not discussing this with you. I was the victim in this, it was my car ruined."

"But I'm being accused of something I didn't do."

His shoulders sagged slightly. "Look, Maisy, if you didn't do it, I'm sure it will be proven. The truth will come out in the end."

"If you believe that, you're even more naïve than I thought."

"Well, anyway, thanks for stopping by. Next time, I call the police," he said, crunching back over the gravel driveway toward the door.

She turned around and walked away. "Prick," she murmured under her breath.

\*\*\*

Maisy was seated at the kitchen table, skimming through the Indeed website yet again.

The front door opened and Ameera walked in, shaking herself off from the rain. "Where ya bin, man?" she called down the hallway.

"I've been busy," Maisy replied, distractedly chewing her nail as she finished yet another application and pressed send.

"Doing what? You just lost your damn job." She walked into the kitchen and stood behind Maisy, peering over her laptop.

Maisy had one knee perched up on the table as she scrolled. "Exactly. I've been applying for loads more jobs on here."

"What kind of thing are you going for?"

"I've applied for marketing, sales, estate agents, a call centre, a coffee shop, all sorts. And the only one I've had a reply back from is a six-month volunteer position."

"Oh c'mon, man, you can't live without pay for six months, there must be something better."

"They cover expenses! The only problem is, it's in Scotland."

"What the hell? Scotland? Now you're just being stupid, man! Tell you want, they've got some jobs at the warehouses in town delivering as a courier. Why don't you do that?"

"I dunno, it might be nice to get away for a few weeks in the Scottish wilderness."

"It's not a holiday!" She started laughing, sounding a tad hysterical. "I tell you what, man, sometimes I wonder about you."

"Thanks for your support, but I'm kidding – I couldn't go that far away." *Could I?*

"Well, you never know. Hopefully one of the other jobs will come through, init. Where are the others? Jordan? Yemen? Switzerland?"

"Now you're being silly; they're all in Leicestershire."

"Well, that's one thing, flipping heck. What else you been doing?"

"I've been to the hospital, applied for a bank loan, oh, and I went to see Michael."

"Woah. Woah. Woah. Take a step back a minute. So, you've finally been into the hospital to see your dad?"

She stared back at her friend. Looked down to her lap. "No. I couldn't do it."

Ameera narrowed her eyes.

"I just kept thinking, what if he blames me? My family are always judging me, and I just don't know how to not react to them. So, I got to the first floor and then I left. You want a coffee?" she asked, standing up and straightening out her cramped leg.

"Go on then. Oh my god, man. Do you want me to come to the hospital with you?"

Maisy shook her head in response; Ameera wasn't stopping for a breath.

"You guys need some kind of family therapy or something. Not that I can talk, my family's jokes, man. Me and my mum ain't even talking right now, I'm sick of all the drama."

"She still hassling you about getting married?"

"It ain't even that though, these guys are upset that I'm working for peanuts whilst I'm trying to get promoted. They think I should be training to be a housewife. Mate, you and me got opposite issues going on. It don't matter," she said, shaking her head. "What you gonna do about your dad, anyways?"

"Nothing now. He should be coming home in the next couple of days," she said, flicking on the kettle and pulling two mugs down from the cupboard.

"Okay, but if you want to face your fears, I'm just saying I'm here."

"I appreciate that."

"And… you went for a bank loan? For the business start-up."

"Yep, I got turned down."

"Why?"

"Cus I'm shit with money and my business plan was crap too; apparently you have to be organised first," she said matter-of-factly, spooning coffee granules into their mugs.

"You should have asked me. I could have helped you. Who's Michael, anyway?"

"Eh?"

"You said you went to Michael's house."

"Oh yeah, my old boss."

Ameera's eyes widened as she took the steaming coffee mug from Maisy. "You went to that Michael's house?"

Maisy sat down at her laptop, hugging one knee to her chest, her coffee mug clutched in the opposite hand. "Yeah, I went to have a look at the car. He saw me on the CCTV and came out to see what I was doing…" She took a sip off the top of her steaming mug.

"Are you flipping mad? Don't go to his house, man. Next thing, he'll be having you done for harassment."

"I didn't get anywhere, anyway."

Ameera paled. "Ah shit, of course he's got camera's, a house that size." She gasped leaning forward in her seat, a pained expression on her face. Maisy turned to look at her, she felt her stomach roll. "He just had it fitted. In case the villain came back. For fuck's sake, Ameera, why do you look so worried? You think I did it too, don't you?"

Ameera gulped and shook her head, her eyes wide. "Of course, not, man. It's not even that deep though, why not just let it go now and move on?"

"I will – I just wanted to know the truth first."

"Well, you might never get it. Just accept it."

Miles walked into the kitchen.

"Miles, don't you think she needs to drop this whole criminal damage thing?"

"Why? What's she doing?"

"She went round to the guy's house."

Miles looked at her in surprise. "You went round to his house? Maisy! Are you mad? Dad's gonna freak."

"No, he won't, because he won't know."

"See, I told you, man, you shouldn't be doing it," Ameera exclaimed.

Maisy's head was beginning to spin. Why was everyone always in her business? "Fine. Fine, drop it now then, please."

"Ugh, I don't know what you were thinking," said Ameera.

Miles opened the cupboard. He pulled out a loaf of bread and several different sandwich meats and cheeses from the fridge. He started sloppily slathering mustard and mayonnaise all over several slices of bread. "Maisy, have you been to see Dad yet?" he asked, spinning the half empty, bread bag round.

"Nope, no point. He'll be home in a few days."

He piled his sandwiches onto the plate and sliced down the middle with a butter knife. "He's been in there for weeks." He looked up at her, a furrow low on his head; he put a can of coke into his jogging bottoms pocket, making them dip. "Never known anyone so selfish as you, Maisy," he grunted. "He's, our dad. Have a little respect."

Maisy opened and shut her mouth like a fish. Miles walked out shaking his head. Ameera sat next to her at the table. "You should have told him. Why didn't you tell him you tried to go in?"

"It doesn't matter. This lot will form their own opinions of me no matter what I do anyway."

"Still should have told him. He's not being fair to you, but he doesn't know you're struggling."

"Ameera! Just let it go. Please."

\*\*\*

Maisy sliced the carrots and dropped them into the boiling pan of water. One sentence from a song by Macklemore, on loop in her head. She was glad her dad was okay, but they were probably going to try and blame her for him being ill in the first place. Like she had somehow given her father a heart attack on purpose. They blamed her for everything. She dropped the last few vegetables into the pan and swept a blob of butter in, off the blade of a knife. She turned the knob down on the oven, picked up her mug of tea and walked over to the dining table where her mum was already sitting. She slid onto the chair propping one knee up against the table.

"How's Dad?"

Her mum's favourite knitted cardigan was wrapped around her so tight that it overlapped both sides. *Had she lost weight?* She was pulling at a loose thread, suddenly seeming older and more fragile than ever.

"He's making a good recovery. But, Maisy, his blood pressure was through the roof. We need to create a calm living environment for him. Next time we might not be so lucky."

*I knew it!* "Oh, so it's me, is it? Me, causing him stress."

"I'm not saying that."

"You're not putting this one on me! It's not my fault Dad's unhealthy. It wouldn't hurt him to stop eating cheeseburgers. Maybe get on a treadmill now and then."

"Maisy!" she snarked. "No one is blaming you."

"That's gaslighting! Pointing that shit at me, then making out I'm imagining it."

"You're impossible! Jesus. I'm just saying he needs calm to get better. Okay?"

"Dad's heart attack scared me too, you know. Have you not even noticed? I've not been out for weeks. I haven't even been drinking."

"I have noticed. But it's not just the partying, Maisy, he needs a calm, positive atmosphere."

"Well, I'm not going to stress him out, am I?" she screeched. She could see her mum tightening her lips, as if to stop herself from speaking. She knew how they all saw her. She'd been hard work when she was younger, she couldn't escape the reproachful way they all viewed her. It was like a cloak she couldn't remove. "Anyway, I probably won't even be here." She took a gulp of tea.

Kathy's head shot up. "What do you mean?"

"After B2B Estates crashed and burned last week, I started looking at other opportunities. That's what dinner is about. I have an announcement to make."

"Oh." Kathy exhaled and began to twiddle her fingers together in her lap.

Maisy's looked over at her mum, her expression

softened. "I do want to be a better person. And for the record, Mum, I swear to you, I did not touch Michael's car."

Her mum looked up at her. "I didn't think you'd do something like that. But I wonder who did?"

"He probably did it himself to get me in trouble."

"I can't see him doing that."

"You don't even know him! You're far too naïve."

"Don't be rude."

"What? You are naïve, you have to admit it, Mum."

"I don't."

"Alright then, you're not. I'm just imagining it. You don't sign up for useless shit you don't need because you can't say no to salespeople at the door. You didn't fall for that period scheme and lose about a grand either, did you, Mother? Of course you didn't."

Her mum stared back at her blankly. *She looks hurt*, she thought.

Miles walked in, grabbed an apple from the fruit bowl, tossed it into the air, then took a bite. Kathy looked up.

"Hey, Miles, how was work?"

He shrugged. "Alright. I was offered a new position."

"Wow, that's brilliant!"

"It is, they want me to be team supervisor."

"Still in the IT department?" she asked with interest.

"Yep."

"I still don't get why a bog roll company needs tech support," scoffed Maisy.

"Are you stupid? They have a call centre with software, they have HR, they have a website. They have records and contracts and suppliers; they have whole teams of accounts staff."

"Well, I bet the department will flourish with you on the job." Kathy gleamed.

*Great. My brother is getting promoted. Now I look even more useless.*

He lifted the lid off the slow cooker and watched the steam release, before inhaling deeply. "What's for dinner, Mum?" he asked.

"Maisy's cooking, not me."

"What?" He laughed, leaning forwards.

"I am."

"Wow, you really are trying to soften them up this time, aren't you?"

"Miles!" pleaded Kathy.

"No, I have something I want to share with you all," Maisy said, "so, I thought it would be nice to make a casserole and sit at the table. And anyway, I've made dinner loads of times!"

"No, you haven't."

"Yes, I have, Miles!"

"When?"

"Stop!" groaned Kathy.

They both stilled. Miles scanned through his phone then looked up. "Oh my god!" he screamed. They both turned to look at him and he patted his thigh with the palm of his hand in an exaggerated manner. "You're making dinner. You've got something to share? You're pregnant, aren't you?"

Maisy gasped.

Robert walked into the room. "Who's pregnant?" he asked.

"Maisy," Miles said matter-of-factly.

"No, I am not!" she snapped.

"So why did you say it, Miles?" Robert grumbled as he hobbled past them, a weaker version of himself.

"He was jumping to conclusions," said Maisy, "as usual."

Robert stopped with his hand on the back of a dinning chair, his chest heaving. He sniffed the air. "Ooh, what's cooking, sugarplum?"

Kathy smiled up at him. "Nothing to do with me, honey bear!"

Maisy and Miles simultaneously screwed up their faces.

"Maisy made dinner for us," Miles quipped. "She," he said, air quoting, "'has news she wants to share'. That's why I think she's preggo."

Robert looked up; his mouth dropped open; the skin under his chin wobbled. "You're not actually pregnant are you, Mais?"

"No, Dad," she snarked.

Miles laughed "Okay. Well then, I'm officially worried."

Maisy looked around at them all incredulously. "You lot act like I don't do anything around here." The room fell silent. She stood up and started banging around, putting plates out and putting food into serving dishes. "Dinner's ready, but I don't know why I bloody bothered."

Kathy looked up at her through her lashes. "Sorry, love, it was just a bit of a surprise, that's all. I can't wait to taste what you made."

"It's not your fault, Mum."

Robert was the last to sit down. "Come on then, we're all ears, Daisy Maisy."

She hated it when he called her that. Pet names were supposed to be a sign of affection, but he only called her it when he was being patronising. *You took a day off school, Daisy Maisy, why is that? Why don't you want to do A-Levels, Daisy Maisy, you won't get anywhere doing an apprenticeship. Why can't you just stick to a job, Daisy Maisy, your mum and I can't support you forever. Uhhhh.*

She placed crockery pots of broad beans and broccoli onto the table, then carried over the huge casserole dish, wobbling as it strained on her fingers. She found a space to put it down.

She stood up straight and glanced over at them all furtively. "So…" She smiled nervously. "I got accepted into the Southfields Group, as a pain volunteer."

Miles glanced over and smirked. "Pain volunteer? What does that entail? Volunteering to be tortured?"

She stared at him, blank-faced. "No, you idiot, I'll be a trained pain specialist. Helping people who need support."

"You! Helping people in pain?" Miles scoffed.

Maisy finished placing casserole on the plates around the table. Everyone was quiet as they filled their dishes with vegetables; she looked around. There was doubt on all of their faces. A few years ago, that probably would have caused her to storm out in an angry rage. This time, she was feeling something else. Something more energising, and she realised that after so many failures, all she wanted now was to prove them all wrong.

"You're going to listen to their problems? And figure out ways to get them help?" Robert asked, covering his scepticism poorly.

"Never mind," she grumbled, shovelling green beans into her mouth and chewing with exaggeration.

"Why, honey? We want to hear," Kathy said softly.

"No, you don't, Mum. And it doesn't matter."

Her mum gave her father a stern look, and he smirked cheekily. "What? What did I do?"

"I'm going to do it whether you lot believe me or not," said Maisy.

"Oh my god, Maisy!" her brother cried, exacerbated. "Why do you have to behave like such a child."

"Oh, I'm the child am I, Miles? Says the one!" She laughed sarcastically and begun imitating his voice. 'Oh, Mummy, I'm selling bog roll, I'm so special I need an award.'"

"Seriously, what is wrong with you?" He gasped.

"Miles, stop," yelled Robert. "But c'mon, Mais, we all know you've tried the whole 'turning-over-a-new-leaf' thing so many times. We just want to make sure you're not being rash."

"I don't care if none of you have faith in me," she snarled, clearly caring. "Anyway, after a two-month online training course, I'll be sent to a live in position for six months in Scotland."

Robert's water burst from his mouth, and they all turned to look at him. "Scotland?" he asked.

She nodded.

"Whereabouts in Scotland?"

"A small town called Illvenie. It's on a mountainside."

"Sweetheart, you do realise that the town is going to be extremely basic, don't you? The Highlands are very rural places." He put his hands out in front of him, as though approaching an angry tiger. "Now, I'm not judging, I'm just making sure you're aware."

"I'm not stupid. I *have* googled it, Dad. It's a tiny, cute village nestled amongst the mountainous countryside. It'll be amazing. I can run a yoga class for locals, try hiking and really be at one with nature."

"And you'll help someone in pain?" he said. "I mean, that's actually why you're going there, isn't it?"

"Well, of course! That goes without saying."

"There will be no one to cook for you."

"Why would I need someone to cook?" she asked, indicating towards the plates with her head and curving her lip in an upward slant.

"There will likely be no shopping centres or those cappulappulattes you like to drink."

"No eyelash extensions, tanning beds or hairdressers I bet," added Miles.

"Plus, Scotland is flipping freezing, and you hate the cold."

"It's Scotland! Not bloody Thailand, Miles, of course they have hairdressers and beauty salons."

"Well, actually, Thailand is more likely…" Robert began.

She cut him off. "Look, do you want me taking responsibility or not? Make up your bloody mind."

"Of course, we do. I just want you to be realistic about it. It will be arduous work; it will be isolating. You will need to be prepared."

She glared at him. "I'm not a bloody idiot," she said through gritted teeth. She jumped up out of her seat, her body rigid. She began grabbing their plates and clanking them together hastily. Miles was still cutting up a piece of meat when she swiped his plate from under him. He stared down at the empty space then up at his sister, his folk poised.

*Oh yeah, moving to Scotland and proving my family wrong is going to be so satisfying.*

# Four

Lizzo was blasting out on the radio as she sped along the A9. She could see the sea in the distance over the hilly coastal road. The music cut off as a call from Ameera came through.

"Hey."

"What's happening, Mais? You coming out tonight?"

"Can't. I'm in Scotland!"

"Ha-ha, very funny!"

"I am. I am currently driving up the A9 coast towards Falkirk."

"Ah, man, so you're actually doing this?"

"Yeah, I'm doing it."

"Shit, I really didn't expect you to follow through with it."

"You and everyone else."

"Nah, man, I'm proud of you, I just don't think it will be what you hope. How did your mum and dad take it?"

"Fine, I just can't wait to prove them all wrong."

"I hope you do, innit. Show them who's boss. I'm just gonna miss my drinking buddy."

"You still have Sasha and Roxie."

"Yeah, but they ain't as crazy as you, though. Roxy is never gonna dance to bhangra around a stranger's car or try to make sweet potato fries in the toaster like we did."

"I ain't as crazy as me no more. We were back in uni then, now we need to grow up."

"Why, man? Growing up is boring. Anyway, it was only last week you gave Miles that cake that was actually a washing-up sponge with frosting on top. And we gave those ugly men Roxy's number pretending it was yours, and that your name was Foxy." She started giggling. "She was so mad! One of them sent her a picture of his…"

"I'm aware!" snapped Maisy, cutting her off. "But that's what I mean, Meer. We can't piss about forever!"

"Fucking hell, you're starting to *sound* like Roxy, and that girl's boring as hell, trust me."

"She's alright."

"Well, you have fun in boring Scotland, anyway. I'll be here getting wasted and having all the real fun, without you. You'll be back before you know it! You forget I know you. Same old Maisy since uni." Maisy heard her gulp before continuing. "Have you heard anything more from the police about the other night?"

"No, I haven't heard anything since, apparently they're investigating it. I've had to leave them my details so that they can get in touch if they need to. My dad said he will deal with it though."

"That's jokes, man. They ain't got any proof to even be blaming you."

"No, but apparently I'm the only person with a motive."

"I bet the guy's got loads of enemies! Oh my god. He's probably making it up, just to get you into trouble."

"That's what I said."

"Too right, I'd have done the same thing, man."

Maisy gulped. "But I didn't do it!"

"Well, as far as we both know!" She laughed. "We were pretty drunk; we could have done anything."

"Stop talking rubbish. We were drunk, we weren't out of it."

"Yeah, you're probably right. Be funny if we did though, wouldn't it."

"No!"

Maisy turned the Mini off the A-road onto a much smaller road, travelling over a tight bridge.

"Either way, I reckon the guy must have deserved it."

"Not really. He was only doing what was right, sacking me."

Ameera started laughing, "Ah, listen yeah, I've got to go. My cousins just got here to go over her wedding plans. She's doing my flipping head in with it all. Love ya."

"*Ciao* for now. Love you."

Maisy rubbed at her tight chest, ignored the heavy feeling against her throat. She knew she hadn't done it, but her gut feeling was wavering; she was questioning her drunken sanity. She followed the directions of the satnav onto a much smaller countryside road. The conversation had her wound up tight. The road suddenly inclined, the gears of her Mini groaned. The satnav led her through two mountains and up into the third.

Maisy was both terrified and in awe of the beautiful scenery of waterfalls, and strange cows with horns and mops of hair on their heads. There was so much greenery and sheer drops where sheep stood sideways. She pondered how they didn't fall. Some parts of the terrain were questionable as to whether her little car would make it. Funnily enough, the six-week online training course she'd had to do in preparation hadn't covered an outdoor survival section.

Several miles along and the road was getting quieter, steeper, and thinner and the satnav went grey, with 'No Connection' stamped on the top of the screen.

"Flipping fantastic," she cried out to the empty car.

There were no other cars on the road; she continued driving straight, hoping the satnav would come back to life. Ahead it looked as though the road was ending. She slowed the car, jabbing at the satnav, the screen started to whir. The female computerised voice made her jump. "Your destination is ahead. The remaining route is a walking path."

Maisy looked ahead, just making out a tiny entrance surrounded by hanging bushes and she felt her pulse quicken. How could she walk that trail alone? It was an old hikers' path, overgrown and close to the edge of a cliff.

Maisy looked back at the map. It was a fifteen-minute walk into Illvenie and there were parking spaces further on. The only other option meant travelling back through the mountains another forty-six miles. By the time she reached Illvenie it would be dark.

She parked the car. As she climbed out and stepped towards the mouth of the cut-through, the chorus of a song by Ed Sheeran was spinning through her head, the same line repeating like a broken record.

She glanced at the screen of her phone. No reception. *Perfect.* She slipped it into her jean pocket. The rocks felt lumpy beneath her Jimmy Choo ballet pumps. She placed her suitcase on the floor, slung her handbag over her chest and set off, dipping under the bush, trudging out onto the rocky trail. The path was thin, rocky, and overgrown with bushes that caught in her hair. But it was either get scraped by bushes or tumble over the sheer drop to her left. Her chest was tightening, her eyes widening, her mouth was dry, and she felt her breaths coming quicker. She marched on, telling herself not to look. Trying to think of things that would distract her mind from the terror she was feeling inside. She fanned at her eyes as they watered, not wanting her lashes to drop out. But there was little she could do to stop the shaking of her legs. When she saw the end of the trail, it took everything in her not to run to it. Carefully, she climbed through the gap in the bush, landing on an old, cobbled road. Ahead, she saw an actual street with buildings. She told herself she was safe and ignored the tightening in her throat, gulping in deep breaths of air.

# Five

Davie Marshall trampled back over the field; his dog, Tennant, followed closely behind. He opened the gate and his eyes flickered to the far end of the road. He stopped in his tracks. A woman was climbing through the hedge of Willie's trail. She had mousey hair all wrapped up on top of her head, like she'd been dragged through a hedge backward. She was slim, about his age, but petite in height. Her skin was soft and peachy, her eyes large and angel-like. She was definitely not from around the Highlands. For a start, she was wearing open-top flats that looked like they were made of fabric and a jacket that looked like it wouldn't keep a person warm indoors on a summer's evening. What kind of an idiot trekked the Highlands in attire like that, with a big bag on flipping wheels. He could tell immediately she was one of them stuck-up Southerners.

It looked as though she'd been crying. There was mascara streaked down her cheeks. His mind skittered scenarios. Had she been hurt? She looked flustered but not distressed. Knowing her type, she'd probably broken a nail and had a breakdown or something.

She straightened up, dropping her bags to the floor. Pink bags with weird jewels hanging from them, he noticed. She put a hand over her diaphragm, and yep, her nails were also long, pink, and jewelled like her bags. She closed her eyes, inhaled then exhaled in a very long, exaggerated manner. Davie leant forward, peering at the woman. *What in hell is she doing?* She lifted her arms over her head, her fingers interlinked above her, her eyes still closed, still breathing deeply, her chest rising and falling. His eyes ran over her breasts, dropped to her taught stomach, thighs, and curvy backside. He gave himself an internal slap as his dick twitched in response. Feeling guilty, he kept his eyes on her face. He'd never seen eyelashes so long.

Her eyes sprang open and landed directly on his. *Ah shit.* He'd been sprung. She gasped. Her eyes widened and for a moment he couldn't draw his eyes from hers. It felt primal as they both stood silently staring, eyes locked, attempting to read one another. The next thing he knew she was hurtling towards him, her hands full of jingling bags. *Fuck!* He cursed to himself. Now he was going to have to talk to the stuck-up cow.

"Excuse me! Excuse me!" she called out in an annoyingly shrill, midlands accent.

*Ugh. What is with this woman. Is she crazy?*

Davie recommenced his walk back up to the village. Maybe if he pretended he hadn't heard her, she'd go away. Like a cow on the field did. But it wasn't long before she caught up to him. Tennant stopped by his feet and looked up at him. He looked down at the dog, then spoke to him from behind his hand. "Watch out, boy, I think we've got a live one."

"Can you help me?" she called, getting blown sideways by a gust of wind.

He frowned at her questioningly.

"I'm looking for Coorie Nook."

His frown deepened. He rubbed the back of his neck and said in a gruff voice, "*Coorie nook* is a 'wee hoose' and there are a few of them around here. Ye ken?"

She frowned back at him and opened her mouth, then snapped it shut. She spoke slower, like she was talking to a caveman. "I'm l-o-o-k-i-n-g for a w-o-m-a-n called A-n-g-i-e, she lives on M-a-i-n S-t-r-e-e-t. The letter said to 'go to C-o-o-r-i-e N-o-o-k', that's where I'll be s-t-o-p-p-i-n-g." She started riffling through one of the many bags, which was straining her fingers.

He tapped his toes on the ground. "Aye, you're talking about Angie Smith. She owns a wee cottage named Corinuck."

"That's what I said, Coorie Nook."

He rubbed his head, beginning to get a headache. "Coorie Nook is not the same as Corinuck," he said, irritated. She was staring at him again, a frown over her saucer sized brown eyes; his resolve softened. She had goosebumps, he noticed. He thought about offering her his jacket but instead picked up two of her bags. "Nee mind. Come on, I'm going past there now, I'll show you."

"Thank you."

"C'mon, Tennant," he called to the dog, stomping ahead.

"Your dog's called Tennant?" she asked. "As in Doctor Who, David Tennant?"

He turned to her and gave her an inquisitive look. "No, not as in bloody Doctor Who. It's a bevi."

"A bevi?"

"Aye, a bitter."

"Oh," she responded.

He stomped ahead; she followed closely behind.

"How do I know you're not a murderer leading me back to your lair?"

He swivelled on her, ready to lash out, but found himself unusually tongue-tied by the innocence in her eyes. *This woman is annoying as hell but also mesmerizingly beautiful.* "You probably should have thought about that 'fore climbing through wee hedges and talking to strange men when there's no one else around," he responded weakly.

"I had no choice. There are no roads leading into this place. I had to ditch my car. What kind of a place has no roads?" she asked curiously.

He continued walking. "Of course there are flipping roads in. What are you, some kind of an idiot? For starters, you're walking on one."

He saw her looking around.

"Yeah but it doesn't lead to the motorway, does it?" she mumbled.

He shook his head in disbelief. "It leads to wherever you drive. That's how roads work."

"Do you always call strangers idiots? I've known you for about five minutes and can already tell you're a rude person. To think, people call me rude sometimes, but I would never call someone who I don't know an idiot just because they happened to park on the wrong side of a village."

She paused and he sighed in relief, until she started jabbering again. "For your information, I'm actually quite smart. I'm not an idiot at all, but it would have taken me another couple of hours to get all the way around to the village that way."

He felt like he needed to scratch his own brain; he'd never heard someone go on so much that it had made his brain physically itch.

He turned around, stunned by her silence. She was looking at him like she was expecting a response. "Aye, that it would. But you'd have your car right now and wouldnee be risking your life walking Willie's trail in cardboard shoes, moaning at a strange man now, would you?"

"I can tell you now that these shoes will have cost more than your whole outfit; they aren't cardboard! And I'm not moaning, I'm just expressing an opinion. What? Is it not okay in Illvenie to express an opinion?"

He scrubbed at his face with clenched fists. "Oh my god!" he growled. "Do you ever flipping shut up? And I didn't ask how much your damn shoes were. They're not suitable for trekking. Your feet must be aching, eh? And you're cold too."

"They are not, and I am warm, thank you."

He knew she was lying, had recognised the pinched look on her face mere minutes before as she'd glared down at them, saw the goosebumps along the peachy skin of her chest. And little did she know, the expensive shoes would be ruined by the time she made it over to the house.

"I guess I'm wrong then," he said, smirking back at her.

"Yes. Yes, you are." She grimaced back.

They walked a little further up the hill.

"My name is Maisy, by the way."

"Aye," he grumbled.

She huffed. "What's yours?"

"Davie."

"And have you lived here long, Davie?" she asked.

"Yep."

"Regular chatter box you are."

"And you're quite annoying, you know that. But I'm not usually one to state the obvious."

"Oh, *annoying*, am I?" she asked, raising her eyebrows.

He grinned to himself. *What a pain in the arse.*

"I've got lots of friends who don't think I'm annoying."

"Good for you. Alright, Maisy, I'll play yer game. What brings you to Illvenie? Fancied a challenge, did ya? Maybe you wanted a bit of fresh Scottish air to fill those lungs. Or did yer family just need a break from you." He saw her flinch at that one. *Bingo!* "Unless – wait a minute… were you specifically sent here to drive me insane?"

He wished he hadn't mentioned the fresh air, instantly the images of her filling her 'lungs' flashed into his mind. He berated himself again. Jesus, he was like a horny teenager.

"My family didn't need a break from me! I needed a break from them, if anything. But that's not why I'm here. I'm here to help Angie and a guy named… Bob. I'm a pain support volunteer."

He stopped in his tracks, turned, and narrowed his eyes at her. "Pain support, you say?"

"Yep."

"You sure?"

"Of course, I'm bloody sure. It's why I've driven over five hundred bloody miles."

He felt a dizziness wash over him. "We're a community. People round these parts, we support each other. Maybe they don't want your help. Have you ever thought of that?"

He saw her bottom lip wobble and her eyes glaze over; he felt the anger dissipate. He was never normally so rude; he didn't know what had got into him.

"Ah, do not start crying. Jeez, if I would have known you'd been so sensitive aboot it, I'd have kept my trap shut. I didn't mean to upset you, okay?"

"I'm not upset."

He grinned, and they stood awkwardly for a moment.

"Can we just get there? I'm exhausted," she said, gesturing up at the small row of houses on Main Street.

He pointed to what looked like a shed in the middle of the field beside them. "We're here, lass," he announced, "Corinuck."

# Six

Maisy stomped across the field, the mud squelching into her shoes. She tried to hold her bags up, avoiding huge cowpats swarmed by tiny brown flies. Why did they even call them pats when they were clearly more liquid than solid? She could feel the bloke's eyes on her, could sense he was still grinning that stupid, condescending grin. *Why had it been him walking up that hill in my time of need. Who did he think he was, anyway?*

The guy was bloody huge; he'd picked up her bags like they were nothing. His huge biceps barely even flexing beneath his flannel shirt. His ruggedness had initially thrown her off guard and her usual witticisms escaped her. She didn't know how to talk to a man like that, the men she knew went to the gym and drank protein shakes to get muscles like his. They got mani-pedis and dressed in brands. This guy probably didn't even know what a brand was, and his muscles and tan were most likely unintentionally from working outdoors. She could literally see the testosterone steaming from his aura.

*He is also blatantly rude.*

She decided in that moment that if she saw him again – once she'd got her bearings back – she was going to lay it on him. How dare he think he could make assumptions about her? She'd never taken shit from a man before and she wasn't about to start. Even if they did look like they could throw her over their shoulder, carry her to the bedroom and do wicked things to her. She felt something wet creeping up her foot. She looked down to see her shoe had sunk into a pile of crap. She was about to scream when she remembered Viking-hillbilly man was still standing behind her. She glanced around; he was watching her, arms folded across his broad chest, leaning back with a look of indulgence on his face. She frowned at him and he winked. *Flipping winked! What an ass.* Slowly, she pulled her foot from the dung and took the last couple of steps with a shudder as her shoe squelched.

She looked at the building, the smell of shit lingering around her nose, and for a minute she wondered if the rude Viking-hillbilly was winding her up. It looked more like a shed that a farmer stored cow feed in than a house. She knocked on the door. No reply. She stood for a moment, listening. She pulled the phone from her jean pocket and looked at the screen; still no reception. She knocked again. He hadn't left; she could still feel his eyes on her, and she couldn't decide if she was turned on or wound up by that. She allowed herself another brief look over her shoulder.

"Just go in. Angie's gone on a market run," he called in that gruff, humorous way.

"I can't just walk in… I'll wait for her." She huffed.

"Just go in, she won't be back until evening."

She put a hand on the doorknob, her chest tightening. She sucked in air. She couldn't fill her lungs.

"Maisy," he called. She turned to look at him. "Trust yourself," he said. "You got all the way here by yourself; I'm assuming you're a capable adult."

She was. She felt a calm wash over her. She was capable, she wasn't an idiot.

"I don't have a key," she snapped.

He dropped his hands to his side, dramatically. "Ah well, why didn't you say? That changes everything then! Just turn the flipping knob. The hoose will be open."

"Wait, you know Angie?"

"Aye, we all know each other round here."

"And you say she'll take hours? At the supermarket?"

"It's in Inverness. A way from here."

"There are no *local* shops?"

She saw him glancing at his watch anxiously. "Just McOwen's, it's a wee all-in-one thingy but it only sells essentials. Look, nee mind that, I canee just leave you standing here in the cold and I'm already late. I've got places to be, you know."

"Just go."

He looked up to the sky. "That wouldn't be very neighbourly of me to do now, would it?"

"I think that ship sailed long ago."

He smirked back at her. She peered into the tiny window nervously. Davie huffed and stomped over. Quickly, she turned the knob, and, to her surprise, the door did open. She let it swing all the way.

"Welcome home," he said, gesturing around with his arm outstretched.

She felt his eyes bore into her. She removed her filthy shoes and stood up. "Don't think I'll ever get these clean again now."

When she stood up, she realised they were jammed in close together. She felt the heat from his big hulk of his chest just inches from her own. She gulped, her eyes lingering over his long wavy dark hair, long beard speckled with red, and his large muscular shoulders. Her hips softened and her pants dampened.

And then he guffawed. "What the flipping hell are you doing, lass?"

"What?" she asked, looking down at her crutch guiltily.

"Why are you taking your shoes off in here?"

She sighed in relief. Her shoes! He was talking about her shoes! "They're covered in cow shit!" she shouted back.

"The house isn't much better," he snarked, the veins straining in his red neck. "You'll get muck all on your bare feet."

"Rather muck than shit!" she shouted into his face. She wasn't even sure why they were both still shouting at each other. But she'd never had so much fun arguing with someone before.

"You clearly know nothing about rural living. What are you, some sort of a city girl?"

"Yes, actually, I am! I don't see why that's anything to be ashamed of. We can't all be hillbillies!"

"Did you just call me a hillbilly? Ach, away with ye, your heid's in the tinny, love."

She felt her lips twitch. She tried her best not to burst into laughter, but she was sure she'd seen a flash of amusement on his face too. If only for a moment. She continued the charade. "I've just met you, and all you seem to want to do is insult me! Is that how you treat all of your guests in these parts? You think you're superior to me because you know how to live in pig filth! Is that what this is?"

He was blatantly watching her, unmistakably grinning.

"What are you fricking smiling at?" she snapped.

"Nothing," he said, looking highly amused. Something twinkled in his eyes.

He turned and looked around the house. She stomped her foot and turned in the same direction, ignoring his close proximity or the charge of electric emanating from him. She placed her hands on her hips and tried to calm her heavy breaths. They both scanned the room awkwardly. *Why couldn't she breathe naturally?* The whole house was the size of her bedroom back home. It was tiny, dull, and cold. There was an open fire, which looked a hundred years old, and the kitchen, lounge and office were all squeezed into one room.

Surely someone couldn't be expected to live there. She opened a door at the back of the room. A bird flew out and she crouched down, letting out a sharp, loud scream.

"Jesus fooking Christ!" Davie screamed back. "It's just a wee bird, for god's sake, woman." He shooed the bird out of the front door whilst she hid behind the kitchen unit, shaking.

She stood up. "Is this some kind of a joke!? There is no way I'm living here." She gathered her bags. "Tell Angie I came, I saw, and I bloody well left."

"Knew someone like you couldn't make it here," he muttered.

She peered up at him, her hands were still shaking, her heart pounding beneath her ribs. "What did you just say?"

His gaze became more intense. "I know your type, Maisy, with your Evian and your damn avocado smash. Bet you order steak in a restaurant but won't go within ten feet of a real cow. Well, city girl, I'm not doing your dirty work for you. If you can't hack the real world, you'll have to speak to Angie yourself."

"You don't even know me to judge me!"

"No, you're right, Maisy, I don't know you. And yet, the moment I met you, I knew you'd run away, give up before you'd even given Illvenie a chance, the wee moment you realised it's no Hilton or Marriott hotel, isn't that funny?"

She didn't know why he was so angry at her but the sound of her name on his angry lips had pulses pounding in places she didn't even know had pulses. She wanted her body to stop reacting. This guy was big, gruff and unstylish. He probably burped and farted as he sat on the sofa watching *Dancing on Ice* with his hands on his crown jewels, she decided. If he even had a TV that was.

She dropped her bags to the floor, her eyes never leaving his as she remembered her family making the same assumptions about her; remembered her words to them as she'd told them she was going to make it work out here. Of course, then, she hadn't known she'd be living like a peasant with a village full of outlanders. Could they survive out here? Without their creature comforts? Probably not.

Davie watched her, then he nodded his head and walked through another door. She followed him wordlessly.

The room had another fireplace, a bed that looked like

it was on the verge of collapsing, and a small white bedside cabinet. She chewed the inside of her lip.

"This room's not so bad, see?" he said, glancing back on her with a nod of his head.

Yes. Yes, it bloody well was. How was she ever going to live there? She couldn't say it aloud, of course, because to Viking-hillbilly it was probably normal to have rabbit poo in your lounge and exposed brickwork everywhere. He would probably just judge her as a prissy city girl. Everyone misunderstood her, the only difference was, this bloke somehow thought his opinions were the only opinions that counted. Sometimes, she just didn't get other people. Her mother treated her like an ornament ready to crack, her father made her feel unskilled and useless. Even her boss Michael had believed her capable of shitting on his car in retaliation for being fired.

She knew why they saw it: she was over-sensitive, fiery, and couldn't control her emotions. That didn't make her a bad person. It just made her volatile. She had to prove them all wrong, she had to sleep out here in the wilderness alone. People did stuff like this all of the time, didn't they? They rarely ever got murdered.

"Speak with Angie. And if you're still not happy, I'll give you a lift back to your car myself, alright?" he said as though reading her mind.

"Maybe I'll feel better once it's had a good clean." The words came from her mouth, but she didn't really believe them.

"Alright then." He sighed, his shoulders sagging in relief, and he turned to walk out of the door. "I'll leave you to get settled in."

She felt a moment of desperation; she didn't want him to leave her there in the house alone, where there could be more rodents or bugs or whatever else. She followed him to the door.

"Wait, do you have a key?" she asked him.

"What for?" He laughed.

"This place."

His lips quirked. "You dunee need a key in these parts, darlin'. There are only 181 people here in Illvenie, and we all grew up together."

"Okay," she replied, nervously looking around for something she could use to block the door when night fell.

His eyes softened on her. "We haven't had any crime here since 1976," he said with a smile. "I think you'll survive."

"Do you know where I need to go to find Angie?" she asked.

He turned, one hand on the handle. "She'll come to you." Their eyes locked; she felt as though he was reading her from the inside. She wanted to look away but was far too proud. "Look, I need to be somewhere. I'll give Angie a call. Have her bring some groceries, bed sheets and towels from town, although I imagine she's already on it."

"Thank you" was all she could manage.

"Aye. We don't get many guests around here," he said with an amused glint in his eye.

She rolled her eyes and turned away. "Can't say I'm surprised." She was opening the oven and peering inside cautiously. She straightened up, expecting him to be gone, but instead he was watching her, a frown on his forehead. When their eyes met again. He seemed to come out of a trance, and he disappeared behind the door. She went to the tiny window and watched as he scurried down the path. This cool, collected man suddenly hurried off skittishly. She wondered if he'd left a woman waiting somewhere for him, and how he'd have to explain that he was gone all of this time helping an out-of-towner.

She picked up her phone and typed out a message to Ameera.

*Only met one person here and he's annoying as shit.*

She sent another.

*Nice to look at though. Also, the place is an absolute dive.*

She sent one to her mum.

*Got here safe, just waiting for the organiser to arrive. xx*

She waited but the grey ticks weren't turning blue. She ran around the house, holding the phone up in the air until she ran into a brick, bashing her ankle. A random brick, sticking out of the wall. She dropped her phone and yelped out loud.

*What on earth is this brick doing here. Shit, what am I even doing here?*

# Seven

After going for his morning run and shower, Davie started sifting through the garage. It was still only 6am; he hadn't slept too well. Corinuck was on his mind. Or was it the woman in it that had bothered him so much? Either way, he felt irritable and uneasy about the whole thing. In addition, he felt guilty for leaving her there. She'd come all the way to help his uncle and he had two perfectly nice spare rooms in his own house. His aunt would have given him a piece of her mind. Reminding him that he should have offered her a warm room. He just didn't want another temporary city woman coming in and messing things up again. But Corinuck wasn't in much of a state for anyone to stop in, let alone a snoot like her. She must have been scared out of her wits through the night, unless she'd left. That too was a strong possibility. He decided that she probably had. Only people from Illvenie seemed to understand Illvenie. Chloe had proven that theory when she'd moved into town hoping to find herself; even his proposal couldn't keep her there. She'd felt suffocated, stifled and before he'd know it, she was gone. Poof. Never to be seen again.

Nope, new girl would be gone soon too.

\*\*\*

On his way to the farmhouse, Davie knocked on the door of Corinuck and, unsurprisingly, found no answer. He peeped in the door. It hadn't been lived in. He wasn't at all surprised that she'd bolted. Women like that always did.

He traipsed up the hill and pushed open the large wooden gates. He walked through the overgrown back garden, into the old farm kitchen. As usual, Bob needed his pain medication before Davie was able to help him out of bed. Afterwards, they'd have a game of chess before he started his rounds on the farm. But when he took Bob into the study, passing by the lounge, they noticed a movement. They both peered in; something was wiggling inside a rolled-up blanket on the sofa.

They stopped by the doorway. "What's that?" whispered Bob.

Davie walked in, signalling for Bob to stay back. He stood above the sofa and poked the blanket. It wiggled some more, then Maisy's head popped out of the side, her face covered in hair. She glared at him.

"What in god's name are you doing here?"

She wiggled up into a sitting position and pushed her hair aside. "I couldn't sleep there in that shed house. The bed doesn't even stand properly."

"Hey, Maisy." Davie turned to see Bob grinning and waving sweetly at the girl. The old man had clearly been sucked in by her beauty. "You two have met?" he asked, trying to hold back a scowl.

"Aye," Bob said chirpily. "Angie brought her round and introduced us last night."

"Did you know she was stopping here?"

"No, but she's very welcome to. Corinuck is in no state for a lass alone."

Davie glared at her then and looked back to Bob. "She canee stop here. She'll be fine over there. Might even toughen the lass up."

Bob glared at him.

Davie relented, "fine, fine. I'll give Alfie a call and rearrange my day. I'll help her fix the place up a bit, okay?"

"Aye, good lad."

"I am sitting right here, you know," called Maisy.

"Aye and don't I bloody know it 'n' all."

She rolled her eyes and laid back into the quilt where she was cocooned. Davie couldn't help but smile. *So, flipping annoying.*

He carried tea around the room to everyone whilst Bob set up the chessboard. When he handed one to Maisy, she smirked at him sarcastically and he gave her a piercing glance. When he went into the study, Bob was smiling but Davie could see the clenched teeth and the look in his eyes every time he moved.

"How are you feeling today?" he asked, sitting down.

"Bloody great!" Always the same response, pain or no pain.

As he took away Bob's pawns with great satisfaction, he watched Maisy talking to Hilda. He couldn't blame her for not wanting to stop there. If anything, making her way to the farmhouse had been resourceful. He wondered if he had any old furniture in the garage. Thinking about it, he was sure he had some curtains and blinds away in the loft that his ex, Chloe, had brought from Inverness when she'd first agreed to move in with him. They might even brighten the old place up. Chole had been an out-of-towner too. At first, it had all seemed so exotic and new to her; in less than a year she'd outgrown the place and him.

"Morning," Angie called as she walked in through the front door. She took Maisy off to the kitchen.

Bob groaned as Davie took away another of his pieces. Hilda was looking out of the front window, her long dress dragging on the floor. She turned to look at them. "You can't let the poor fellow win for once?"

Davie gave her an amused look. "'Fraid not. I had to lose to this asshole all through my childhood. I'm not going to let him win now that I can actually beat him, am I?"

"Fair enough." She grinned and nodded.

He took another piece off the board. "Hey, Bob, you don't happen to have any household stuff you're in need of clearing out now do you?"

Bob looked up at him, deep in thought. "What is it you're after, Davie?"

Davie explained that it was for Maisy and before he knew it, Bob, Hugh and Hilda were barking commands at him, places he could find their old things. By lunch, his flatbed was full of old furniture that just needed a lick of paint or a wipe down. Boxes full of fabrics, lampshades, pots and pans that he was sure would be useful. Once Bob was settled, Davie went home to fetch his toolbox, alongside some planks of wood and a couple of pots of white paint. Then he went to the loft for the pink curtains and blinds. Amongst them, he found his mum's old rug and some picture frames that he thought might help.

He piled everything into his old flatbed and tied them in, then he pulled off his jumper. Despite it being only eight degrees outside, he was starting to sweat. He poked his head into the kitchen where Maisy and Angie were seated, going over spreadsheets. When he walked in, he caught Maisy's eyes as they ran over his shoulders and chest. He quickly looked away, not wanting her to know he'd seen.

"I'll go and get started on the hoose," he said, looking at Angie.

Angie nodded, deep in concentration, her glasses balanced on the end of her nose as she scanned spreadsheets.

***

Davie opened the door to Corinuck. Maisy's bags were sprawled out on the kitchen floor, one of them open with clothes spilling out. He tucked them safely into the cupboard, carrying everything in from the van. Then he started rubbing down the walls and filling in holes. Within hours, neighbours were turning up to donate washing machines, dishwashers, dining tables and blankets. Offering their help. Alfie even turned up with firewood and offered to sweep the chimney.

Maisy and Angie arrived later in the day with a bunch of cleaning products from the store. She looked taken aback at how much they'd done and for a moment he wondered if she was going to cry again. But then she surprised him with a sweet smile. She snapped on a pair of rubber gloves and joined in with the graft. Scrubbing floors and cupboards, rubbing down the furniture with sandpaper, ready to be painted.

He finished filling holes in the wall and sanded them down.

"What's this?"

He turned around. Maisy was swinging his caulk from her finger.

"That's caulk. It fills the holes."

She nodded and watched as he opened a pot of paint and poured it into the tray.

"Could I have a go at that?"

"Painting?"

"Yes."

"You can paint the whole lot for all I care."

"But how do you stop it from having lines when it dries."

"It's the drips you want to worry about."

She dipped the brush into the paint and began brushing. He watched as the paint ran along her index finger and dripped from her wrist onto the floor. He chuckled to himself. She turned to him and whined. "This is going to take forever. I'm getting arm ache already."

"That's what rollers are for."

She picked it up and dipped it into the paint, a curious look on her face. "Why didn't you tell me? This is loads better."

"You've never painted before, have you?"

"Nope, never."

"Your parents never showed you?"

"No. My mum's a timid little thing, afraid to get her

hands dirty and my dad used to build houses when I was a child. Never seen him paint though."

"He stopped building houses?"

"Yep. Now he has other people build the houses for him."

"Ah, I see."

Davie picked up the saturated brush, gave it a wipe with a discarded piece of rag by Maisy's feet. He could smell her citrusy perfume drafting from her as she waved the roller up and down the wall, her whole body moving with it. He stood up, dipped the brush and begun running it around the edges.

"What made you want to come to Scotland to volunteer anyway?" he asked. He watched as she chewed her lip, realising there was more to her than he had initially assumed. "You don't have to answer," he said. "Just making conversation."

She stopped the ridiculous squatting and slowly grinned at him. "It's okay, I'm thinking of how to put it."

He gave her time, watching as she silently swept the roller up and down again, panting slightly.

"Sometimes," she mused, "I watch people. Girls in groups of friends, families or people in relationships who seem to really understand each other. Like them couples who really seem to be able to talk to one another without actually talking. You know what I mean?"

He nodded, unsure of where she was going with it.

She remembered trying to join in at school sports, feeling like the odd one out; watching her family communicate, feeling like she wasn't part of the same family. She remembered how getting drunk with Ameera and Roxy or locking herself away with a good book or horror movie were the only places she didn't feel like a misfit. And she said, "I only truly feel comfortable around people who aren't particularly succeeding at life, even though I want to be a better person."

He nodded his head, careful to listen, to not try to fix her problem.

"Now, I feel like the people around me are either expecting me to fail or they're constantly reminding me of my past failings, even if they don't mean to."

He frowned at her. "So, you came away. Where no one knows you?"

"Yes." She nodded.

He smiled back. "You've come to the right place."

"What's your story?"

"I haven't really got one. I grew up with a single mother who was also an alcoholic. We lived in Glasgow, on the poverty line. Once I was here, and I started to get comfy, I felt this massive weight to prove myself. I wasn't the same, but always felt a little like I wasn't worthy. Until I gave in to the Illvenie way."

She was staring at him wide-eyed. Then she blew a loud breath through her lips and beamed.

"Well, I didn't expect that! Jeez, Davie!" She scoffed.

He shrugged his shoulders and smirked back.

They stood in silence for a moment, both painting quietly in rhythm.

\*\*\*

The conversation replayed in his head. Had he revealed too much of himself? These days, he barely even acknowledged a life before Illvenie, let alone openly told someone else about it.

They turned to each other; his eyes travelled over her face and over her lips. She was covered in splatters of paint. One landed right on the end of her nose, and he saw her go cross-eyed as she spotted it too. He was trying not to laugh, but she'd noticed.

"Are you laughing at me?" Maisy asked, eyes wide.

"God no, well yes, actually. But only because you have a little something there." He smirked, pointing at her nose.

"I thought I saw something," she said.

"And here," Davie said.

"Here?" she asked, smearing paint over her chin with her thumb. He couldn't stop the laughter then.

"I'm sorry, I'm not laughing at you." He chuckled, still trying to hold it in.

"Then why are you laughing?"

His shoulders shrugged up and down. He bent over and picked up a paint scraper, turning the aluminium towards her face. "Because your whole damn face is smothered in paint, Maisy. How are you not feeling that?" He laughed and she swiped at him letting out a giggle.

She looked down at her hands then. "Aww I lost a nail!" she whined, and they both burst into laughter then.

Once they'd cleaned up the materials, he plumbed in the washing machine and showed her how to use it. It was clear the city girl was accustomed to having people do stuff for her. And even though he assumed she lived in a beautiful house, she seemed to be enjoying herself there, putting together the barn house. He watched how she looked around at everyone with a massive grin on her face.

He snuck up behind her. "It's the joy of living in a small community. We all help each other around here, lass. You might not be used to it, but this is how us hillbillies do it." He grinned. She looked back at him and smiled, the most natural and relaxed he'd seen her yet.

As Alfie helped him screed the floor, he looked up at Maisy. She had a sponge and was blotching the wet paint from a bookcase, giving it a new/old kind of finish.

"Seems you're going above and beyond for this girl," murmured Alfie.

He looked back up at her and caught her eye before responding. "Don't get any ideas, Alfie. She's an out-of-towner and hasn't had to work a day in her life. She has fake eyelashes, nails and what-not and she's temporary. She's everything I dislike in a woman."

Alfie grinned. "And yet… you can't take your eyes of off her."

"Pah!"

Alfie wasn't far wrong, but he'd never be able to admit that aloud. Maybe it was the way she'd stripped him down, not caring what he thought, or the fact that beneath the angry temper he enjoyed so much, he could see a vulnerable, caring woman. Maybe it was her huge brown eyes, or the way her hair curved up and looped down, falling onto her forehead, forcing her to keep blowing it away. He wasn't sure, but something inside was telling him to give her a chance. And to give her a chance, she needed to want to stay.

The old place was coming together nicely. As the sky darkened, the neighbours dwindled home to deal with their own families and responsibilities. Davie put together some drawers and hung a few shelves. He put up new splash-back tiles in the kitchen and gulped back a glass of icy water. It was just the two of them then. Maisy was on a stepladder by the front door, hanging a pair of curtains, her leggings tight on her arse. As she reached up, he couldn't help but check out the flex of her bum cheek. Good god, he pictured himself covering her arse with his hands and pulling her body into his.

She turned and glanced at him, as though sensing his thoughts. He quickly turned away, noticing the look in her eye. She'd caught him looking, leering even, but if he wasn't mistaken – she'd looked almost pleased. She glanced away and he looked back. She dropped a hook and went to bend over and get it. He dived at the hook, grabbing it off the floor but in the process almost knocking over the ladder. She gave him a quizzical look. He didn't care. Watching her bend over would have killed him where he stood. Had it been intentional? He wasn't sure, but he couldn't get involved. She was temporary. At least this time he was fully aware that this girl was leaving. Chloe had made him think that she had wanted to stay. Made him believe that he was enough as he'd fallen head over heels. Maisy was clear. She was here for only six months. He was mesmerised by every part of her; all he'd dreamed about the night before, were situations and places they'd met and inevitably ended up rolling around, skin-to-skin, but he certainly wasn't a fuck-and-chuck sort of guy, and he wasn't into pretentious women. Nope, he would never go near her, not in a million years.

He glanced at his watch, if nothing else for somewhere to avert his eyes, something to take his attention away from his spiralling thoughts. *It's just lust. That is all, it will soon go.* It was 10pm. 10.02pm to be exact. He looked around. They'd really done themselves proud this time. The fire was blazing, his mum's old large colourful rug covering the concrete floor in front of it. Beside it stood a huge wooden elephant. He really knew absolutely nothing about home décor or interior design but as he stood back and marvelled at it, even he noticed how homey it all felt. Maisy was standing by his side and if he wasn't mistaken, she too seemed impressed. He was starting to see a softer side to her.

He looked around and when he turned back to her, she was watching him curiously. "I cannot believe how much has been accomplished today." She sighed.

He grinned. She really was impressed.

"Yeah, well, I didn't do it for you," he said with a wink. "Bob needs medication and you're the one that's going to report back to the big wigs to get him the help he needs."

She stared at him and for a moment; her facial expression confused him. Was that disappointment? Whatever it was, she'd quickly switched it off. "He means a lot to you, doesn't he?" she asked, surprising him again.

"Absolutely. He was like a father to me growing up. He's been given so many false promises. And as of yet, every out-of-towner has let him down. I don't expect anything different from you, quite frankly."

He saw her flinch. What was wrong with him? Every time he was around her, he seemed to speak his mind without concern for the consequences or her feelings. Now she was smiling at him, pretending his words hadn't made her feel inadequate.

# Eight

It wasn't the sound of the rain beating down on the tin roof, nor was it the owls screeching into the night that had her hiding behind the bedroom wall, quaking in her fluffy socks. It was the cracking of twigs and the loud incoherent echoey sound. Like a combination of a giant frog and a lion. Was that a thing? In Scotland could a frog and a lion mate, creating something ferocious. She imagined a giant frog sitting in the dark eating anyone that happened to pass by. Jesus Christ, what was she thinking? She was losing her mind through lack of sleep and fear, she had to be. *Why have I put myself here in this position?* She couldn't even get away; she'd probably be in more danger walking outside into the dark night, but she had no phone signal to ring anyone. So, in fact, she would have to sit and wait for whatever was out there to come into the unlocked door and eat her.

*Ooh, get a grip, get a grip. Nothing is coming to get you!* she sang a non-descriptive tune in her head, trying to block out her thoughts of what was probably only inches away, behind mere bricks and mortar.

Her mouth was dry. She stood up on her wobbly legs and walked into the kitchen to fetch a glass of water. She moved forward in a squat, avoiding the gap in the kitchen curtain. She gulped, poured herself a glass, and swigged it down, willing herself not to think about outside. She checked that the dining chair she'd wedged under the front door was still sufficiently wedged and she rubbed her hands in front of the smouldering fire. The sound came again. She jumped into the air, holding the scream inside. Shakily, she placed the empty glass back onto the counter. Then paused. Was it closer? She tip-toed out of the kitchen and dived into her bed, shivering. She couldn't decide if the violent shivers came from the chilly night air or the thoughts of being eaten alive by the Scottish wilderness. She imaged a lion prowling around her tiny little house in the dark, smelling the flesh of a human, and she tucked herself all the way under the covers. Tomorrow, she was going home, she shouldn't have gone there in the first place; how stupid of her. She couldn't possibly endure this for another night. It was freezing, the springs of the bed stuck into her, and the animals wanted to eat her. First thing in the morning, she would pack up her things and leave to go home.

\*\*\*

Maisy opened her eyes, peeking up above the covers. Daylight shone through the curtains.

"I made it! I bloody made it," she murmured to herself. She pulled back the cover then shrieked at the frigid air and wrapped herself back up again. She grabbed her phone from the floor beside her. It was 6.36am.

She felt a sense of pride bloom through her. She wiggled her toes outside of the covers, then urged herself all the way out, hoping from one foot to the other. She took a quick hot shower and dressed as quickly as possible. If she went home after only two nights, her family would see it as a failure – dousing the pride she felt for lasting out the night. They would never see what she had accomplished. She'd like to see them withstand it alone. Nope, she couldn't and wouldn't go home yet. One more night wouldn't hurt. It hadn't been that bad. Had it?

# Nine

When he walked in, he could hear her voice. He stood behind the shelf, pretending to look at envelopes. Joan's voice was on-edge as she answered her barrage of questions.

"Can't we get them quicker?"

"Well, no, that would mean one of us driving miles for one or two prescriptions at a time. We wait until we have at least ten and do a run. It's only usually a day or two."

"I was told a lady on Gravel-pit Lane waited five days for antibiotics."

"Sarah? Yes, well, that was because her doctor wrote the prescription out wrong and we had to wait for another."

"So, if you get the wrong prescriptions, you have to wait for the next run? Is there no way of doing a video call with the doctors. Double referencing everything you have?"

"Doctors don't have time for that. They barely have time for appointments," she scoffed.

"What if they need medication earlier?"

"People can go themselves to collect."

"That doesn't seem like it would always be feasible."

She was giving Joan a hard time; she wouldn't understand a community like theirs, but she may well give them food for thought.

"Why don't you share this responsibility wider?"

"Like?"

"Like have a prescription post box, and when another villager travels to Inverness, they take whatever is in the box. I'm sure there must be people that work there on a daily basis."

"There's some. But there's a wee thing called data protection."

"Why is that a concern if everyone agrees to it?"

"It's patient privacy. And what about addiction issues. They don't just give pills to anyone; you're talking strong painkillers, antidepressants, muscle relaxants. The person collecting must be authorised, DBS-checked and monitored."

"Do residents have addiction issues here? I was told Illvenie is basically crime free."

"It is, yes, but we don't want to create issues now, do we?"

"No, just let people die because they don't get their prescriptions in time." Maisy's voice dripped with sarcasm.

Joan folded her arms, inhaling deeply. "What do you propose we do, Miss Fowler?"

"On the spot, I'd suggest: more people authorised to collect prescriptions, with some kind of a flow chart or tick list. That way it can be done several times a day, without bringing back incorrect tablets."

"It's not that easy."

"I'm sure it's not easy for someone in pain either."

Davie made a loud cough.

She turned slowly, looking at him coolly.

"Oh, you."

He was taken back for a moment. He stepped forward.

"Why are you accepting this?" she turned her anger onto him.

He stopped mid-step and looked at her, amused. Was she blaming him? "We're a small community living off the beaten track. There's only so much we can do."

"But what if someone gets an infection or something?"

"That's what immune systems are for."

Her face angered. "Did you know that 123,000 people in the UK get sepsis each year."

He flinched at that.

"One in five of those people die."

Davie glared at her; his jaw tightened. He looked up at Joan behind the counter, she looked like a rabbit in headlights. His throat restricted.

"I'll come back later," he growled before walking out.

She turned back to Joan. "What's his problem?" he heard her say.

As he stomped down the road, his breathing calmed. He wanted to go back for Hugh's tablets. But if he waited just ten minutes, he was sure she'd be gone. He sat down on the Smiths' front wall, giving himself a minute.

When he looked up, feeling much calmer, Angie was approaching, walking up the hill. All dressed in blue with a thick gilet and wellington boots, she spotted him and walked over. She looked at him, concerned, then sat down beside him on the wall.

"Girl got you hot under the collar?" she asked, nudging him playfully.

He looked around, wondering how she knew it was Maisy that was causing him grief.

"I could tell from the moment I met her she'd be your type. Pretty and argumentative," she said with an affectionate smile.

"What makes you think she's argumentative?"

"She's got that angry spark in her eyes. Like someone used to getting their way."

"Oh, and you think I like that in a woman? Pah!"

"I think you can see the potential in that spark. Carey was argumentative, but she was also smart and passionate about the things she loved. Including you."

He beamed at that. "She was kick-ass, she kept everyone in line. Remember when Alfie was thinking about leaving Jo? She soon put him in his place." He laughed.

"Oh yes."

He smiled. "But this isn't about that, Ang. That woman is in McCowens' right now complaining to Joan. Poor Joan looks scared out of her wits."

"Are you kidding me? That woman might look timid, but she's got a bite that stings, Davie. Don't you worry about Joan, she can hold her own."

"It's not just that. She was going on about sepsis." He gulped the word with the imaginary lump in his throat.

Angie's eyes crinkled. She leaned into him. "Oh, laddie, I am so sorry. The lass doesnee know."

"I know she doesn't, it was the only thing stopping me from going off at her."

"She is focusing on helping Bob. You and I both know he needs more help. He's in agony."

"I know but she's barking up the wrong tree… does she not realise brash is how we work. Ahh, nay mind, she's just got under my skin a bit, that's all."

She turned to him, raised her eyebrows, and smirked.

"Oh, don't look at me like that."

"You can't deny she's very attractive."

"Aye to look at she's a flipping goddess. The sooner she leaves the village the better." He grinned.

"Well, you've certainly put the work in to help her stay," she said with a lopsided smile.

"I'm just that kind of a man."

She laughed. "I, for one, am glad you are. I need the girl's help. But what are we gonna do with you, aye, laddie?"

He shrugged.

She winced as she stood back up and pushed her hands into the base of her back. "I've got a good feeling about this one," she said, hobbling off up the hill.

"While you're in the shop, can you grab Hugh's prescription?"

She gave him a look of disgust. "Wimp."

"Aye. And while you're at it, Ang, get you-self some of that Deep Heat for your back."

"Ach!" she grumbled, hobbling away.

# Ten

Maisy walked beside Angie. "We'll be spending the day at Looch Farm today." Maisy nodded and smiled as they walked up the hill together. "I'll get you some wellies whilst we're there. Bob has loads of old ones lying around."

"Okay, thanks." The idea of wearing someone else boots, didn't exactly appeal to her.

"Are Bob, Hilda, and Hugh family?" She asked.

"No, it's Bob's farm. When his wife Carey died, the three of them just kind of ended up clumped together. They're like the Raggy Dolls of Illvenie."

"Raggy Dolls?"

Angie smirked at her. "N'er mind, ya wee bairn."

"So, you're a nurse?"

"Oh no, as a village we have a rota for certain jobs. I looked after the old, sick and infirm a few times and it just kind of… stuck."

Maisy smiled at Angie. "You've given up your own life to care for them? Isn't that a lot?"

"I don't see it as a sacrifice, if that's what you mean."

*How did people use up all of their time on others, give up on their own dreams, and not see it as a sacrifice*, she wondered.

A pair of men stood at the side of the road, leaning against a tractor, talking amiably. They stopped talking and turned. One of them tipped his hat. "Angie, Maisy."

"Hey, Grahame, Alfie," Angie replied.

Maisy smiled, then turned back to Angie, wide-eyed. "How do they know my name?"

"My darling, you're not in the city now. You're in a village of only 180-odd occupants – we all know everyone who comes and goes. Plus, if you dinnee notice, Alfie was in your hoose last night helping."

"He was?"

"He was. He cleaned the chimney! Then he put down new floor tiles."

"Oh, now I remember!" she said. She pictured the man crouched down on the floor with his T-shirt half up his back, a hairy butt crack on full display, and she shuddered.

"But, honestly, darling, no business is your own anymore."

Maisy grinned. She had no idea what the woman was on about, but she didn't care, she liked the idea of being a part of something. Like she belonged somewhere. She knew eventually they'd realise she didn't belong, but for now, she was going to enjoy being part of the community.

Angie opened a wooden gate with a gold plaque that read 'Bob and Carey McAllen's Farm' and underneath, scratched in tiny writing, was a name. She leaned in close. It read, 'Davie'. Angie led Maisy into a courtyard with an overgrown garden, a weedy driveway, and a huge, weathered grey-and-black ornament planted in the middle. She glanced around.

"Used to be a beautiful garden; Carey loved planting flowers of all kinds. Unfortunately, that's the reason it's so overgrown now. Too much regrowth with no one to care for it."

They stepped into the farmhouse kitchen. Boots of all sizes lined up by the door, crusted in dry old mud. She hadn't remembered seeing them the night before. They walked through the hallway, it smelt like old books and cottage pie. Angie led Maisy into the library with huge leather chairs and shelves full of brown leather-bound books.

When she walked in, Hugh was sitting in the corner, a magnifying glass clipped inside the book he held onto, his legs crossed. Bob was sitting in his wheelchair at a table, a book lay spread open as he read.

"Good morning," Angie called.

They both gave her acknowledging grunts.

Hugh had his head dipped low; he raised an arm in gesture.

They approached Bob. Maisy sat down.

"So, you're here to evaluate me today, are you?"

"I am indeed. None of this is new to you is it, Bob?"

"'Fraid not, lass. However, I doubt you'll find a secret potion – I've tried them all. Opioids, analgesics, acupuncture, cold therapy, the lot. Nothing seems to take away my pain. Nowadays, of course, they call it fibromyalgia, but I have not walked more than a few metres since I was cleared of cancer fifteen years ago. Personally, I think it was all the chemicals they used to treat me. Blasts your body through the stuff does, ya know; kills your cells. Mind-ee, without it I may not have lived to tell the tale, eh?"

Maisy grinned and nodded; she didn't know how to respond. Was always one step behind trying to figure out what he'd said in his last sentence.

*Maybe I just have a low IQ.*

"At least then I'd be with my Carey," she heard him murmur into the quiet.

"Where's our Hilda?" asked Angie, walking into the room.

"I think she's sitting in the conservatory. Her grandson travelled up from Inverness, brought with him his wee Jack Russell," Maisy heard Bob telling Angie, but Maisy was still sitting on his last comment.

*How sad, that life doesn't feel worth living without his wife.*

After spending some time talking to Bob and making notes about his pain, his cancer treatment, and the numerous tablets he'd tried in the past, she tried some of the physio exercises she'd been taught. Some she was sure she'd got wrong, but Bob didn't seem to notice or mind.

Maisy was feeling overwhelmed and exhausted from trying to decipher his very strong accent, from trying to figure out the source of his pain. Angie walked over and placed a coffee in Maisy's hand.

"Ready to take a wee walk around the property?" she asked.

Maisy nodded then looked to Bob. "It was nice speaking with you." She began to stand.

Bob smiled. "It was lovely speaking to you too."

She walked out into the high-ceilinged entrance. To her left was a grand stairway that curved out the width of a room. Along the corridors were room after room all decorated in browns with images of pheasants and men in stuffy suits with guns pointed high.

"Wow," she murmured. "I didn't see any of this yesterday."

"Looks like something from a time warp, doesn't it?" Angie said, grinning.

Maisy turned to her and nodded. "It's certainly been kept in good condition."

"Have you seen the lounge?"

"Yes." She smiled. So apparently no one had told Angie she'd slept there the first night.

They walked further into the garden; she could see how it had once been set out with massive displays of flowers. She could imagine all the different sprays of colours and neatly trimmed edges before it had become neglected and battered by the cold Scottish winters.

Angie explained the level of pain Bob was in, his inability to use his legs, how his muscles had begun to deteriorate despite the doctors not seeing anything physically wrong with him.

"Now you've had a chance to meet Bob, any thoughts on a plan for his recovery?" she asked.

Maisy wondered if this is where they would realise she had no skills and send her packing. How could she honestly help him? If she lied – he could end up in even worse pain. And no matter how badly she didn't want to go home with her tail between her legs, she couldn't possibly be the reason he suffered even more…

"Honestly?" she asked taking a deep breath in, preparing herself to be fired again. "I don't see how I can be of help to him."

Angie's eyes widened in response; her eyebrows flew up into her fringe.

Maisy started to regret the words as they were partially from her lips, but there was no going back. "I'm so sorry. I just think I'll be a waste of your time, effort and however much it costs the company to keep me here."

"Why do you say that?" Angie asked softly.

Because for once she wanted to be honest. Because she didn't want to market herself and let these lovely people down.

"Because it sounds like he has something deeply medical going on. Chronic pain for fifteen years! I'm not a doctor, I'm nothing. How could I possibly be of any help to him?"

Angie turned and faced her then. She placed a hand on Maisy's arm, instantly warming her.

"Oh, my darling, you are exactly what Bob needs, you just don't see it yet." Maisy felt herself tighten.

*Why would Angie think that? Had she got the wrong CV?*

"Don't look so worried!" She chortled. "I just watched you sit and listen to that man talk for hours, with interest and compassion. That's the exact opposite of nothing."

Maisy frowned. "Huh?"

"Maisy, many people dismiss the elderly because they just don't have time for them. Or it can be harder for people to talk to those close to them, they somehow feel more vulnerable if they hand over all of themselves to the ones that know them best."

Maisy started thinking about her own family. How she'd often got angry when she'd felt invaded or misunderstood by them. Was that why she found it so hard to admit what she was feeling and instead pointed anger towards them?

"The elderly might often go round the houses, repeat themselves and even get stuck mid-sentence, unable to finish or explain correctly what it is they want to say. Listening takes a certain type of patience. And that's without the language barrier you had to deal with! But sometimes just talking through emotional pain can heal physical pain immensely. And from spending time with Bob, I think that's where his pain stems."

"Oh." She gasped. "From losing his wife Carey?"

"The love of that man's life," she mused. They smirked at each other. "With that in mind, I believe your plan should be to – yes, reassess his medication, research it, do what you can and keep up his physio. But also, I'd like you to concentrate on what you clearly do so well… actively listening. Take note and if anything crops up that you feel might benefit him, then feed it back to me. If you can, ask open-ended questions that will get him thinking and talking more."

Maisy almost laughed. She'd never been accused of being a good listener before. But she could do it. It was within her power to listen, to show empathy and make sure Bob got everything out of his system. She would make sure she did it.

"Now, that I can do," she replied with a grin. She liked the idea that she could help Bob in such a simple way.

A tiny white dog ran over to Maisy; it began growling furiously. She cooed. "Ahh, how cute are you? You angry little thing."

"Thank you," said a male voice. "But my bark's worse than my bite, honestly."

Angie picked the dog up and gave it a cuddle. "Maisy, this is Logan, and this is his dog JD. Logan, this is Maisy. She's here to help Bob with his pain management."

The man approached them; he had large shoulders and thighs with a heavy-set jawline and curly brown hair. He was wearing a shirt with the collar popped and Ralph Lauren shorts, with Ray-Bans on top of his head.

"Hello there, pain lady Maisy," he said, giving her a big smile. He shook her hand; his own hands were hot and beefy, and they swallowed hers.

"Hi, nice to meet you."

"Even better to meet you," he said, holding eye contact with her, giving her a fuck-me grin.

"I'm just going to check on Hugh whilst you two get acquainted," said Angie, moving away and sweeping Maisy's elbow supportively.

Maisy looked around awkwardly. "Why does everyone around here name their dogs after booze?"

"God, I'm not from around here!" He gasped, placing a hand on his chest. "Do I look like I'm from Illvenie?"

She looked at his clothes, her eyes running down to his feet. White crocs. She stifled a giggle. "Actually, you don't," she said, grinning.

"Thank goodness for that. I was about to go and change my whole wardrobe. I'm from Inverness. I think I'd die if I got stuck here." He smirked, looking around and she thought it was ironic that he seemed to think he was above this hard-working village of people in his brands, with his crocs. After a moment, he suddenly laughed. "Oh, no disrespect to the people here *like*. I meant growing up as a teenager. Trust me to put my foot in my mouth with the first beautiful woman I meet in a long time. How long are you here for?"

Maisy laughed; she couldn't remember the last time someone had called her beautiful. When men flirted, they usually just asked for her snapchat. And this bloke was clearly flirting.

"I'm here for six months," she said.

"Six months, eh?" He looked her up and down, as though the idea excited him. She wondered if he had a thing for 'strange'.

They grinned at each other. "I can tell from the way you dress that you aren't actually from around here," she said, feeling at a loss for words. *Wait, have I already said that?* she wondered.

"Is it the shorts?" He grimaced. "It is, isn't it. They're just so damn comfy."

She grinned back at him. "Nah, it's the brands."

"Oh aye, it's like a time warp around these parts. My granny seems to like it though."

"It's a little old fashioned, but I'm beginning to see the appeal of small-community living."

"Who are you trying to convince? Me or yourself?" He laughed and his whole face seemed to open.

She giggled. "What? I'm serious!"

"Course you are," he said with another flash of his perfectly white teeth.

"So, what brings you here?" she asked.

"My granny. Mabel. I check on her weekly. Bring her new magazines and bits. Bring JD to visit her."

"Ah I love Mabel!"

"Now I know you're a liar." He laughed. "She's the rudest old lady I know."

"She's not so bad. I think she's funny."

"Then you're hired."

She laughed. "I'm already hired."

"Then Angie made the right decision. If you like my granny, you're capable of anything."

She started to think. "Hang on! You come from Inverness weekly?" she asked.

He looked at her suspiciously. "Mostly, yes. Why? What's that expression?"

"Would you ever consider maybe doing a weekly shopping-run for these guys?"

He folded his arms and bit his bottom lip as though in thought. "Absolutely I would."

She felt the excitement build.

"Only thing is," he said with a sigh, "it's not always a guarantee when I can get here. My work pulls me around. I wouldn't want to let anyone down by not getting here, you understand?"

"I see."

She felt the disappointment settle.

"Sorry. If I could, I would have loved to help you out."

"Yeah, I get it," she said, wondering if she really did get it.

"Well, if you want to escape back to the real world for a bit tonight, I can take you out for dinner in Inverness."

"You'd drive all the way to Inverness and back here again after?"

He stared at her for a moment as though contemplating something. "It's a two-hour journey. Not the other side of the planet." And yet he couldn't do it to help the community… He was thirsty, it was written all over his face. What had he been contemplating, a hotel? Maybe she'd have gone for it if it meant her not stopping in that shack for another night. Scratch that, even giant hungry frogs wouldn't make her want to sleep with a guy who wore shorts all year round with Crocs. Sure, he was her type in some ways – he was attractive and clearly came from money. A few months ago, she'd have probably gone for it. But there was something about him that she didn't like. He seemed kind of smarmy. She wasn't feeling it –that excitement of being chatted-up by a hot guy. She could see he wanted her and normally it would have been a turn-on, but in that moment, she couldn't care less.

"So?" he asked, his head tilted, eyes narrowed. He might as well have licked his lips at that point. She was preparing to turn him down.

"There's a nice seafood restaurant I like to go to. It's on the coast and has the freshest fish you've ever tasted. Of course, if you have more important plans, don't worry. I mean, for all I know you might be watching the cows with Alfie or on a girls' night dancing in the Bull's Head with Angie, or maybe you're watching Outlander with Davie?"

Her head shot up then. He winked. Maisy laughed and smacked him, playfully. She glanced into the kitchen window – Davie was playing chess with Bob.

"I'm kidding," he said, "but consider it a welcome to the village. No intentions, just two new friends getting to know each other." Her body was reacting now, but it wasn't to Logan, it was the mention and sight of Davie.

"But Davie does look like a Viking; it's funny you mentioned Outlander too."

"Oh, I used to tease my sister about him being a bit of a Neanderthal all the time."

"Your sister?"

"Yeah, you've probably heard her mentioned; Chloe was the one who broke Davie's heart. They were together for a long time. She moved up here. Soon realised there were no opportunities and nothing to do and she left. Everyone around here might as well have pulled out the pitchforks, they hated her for hurting their little Davie."

"And Davie wouldn't leave to be with her?"

"Nope, some people are just stuck in their ways, I suppose. So anyway, you in or not?"

Was this the only local who would feed her info on Davie freely?

"I have some studying to do. But you can pick me up at five," she said with a smile.

Maisy walked back through the main entrance. *So, Davie was in love with Logan's sister. A fellow city girl. Interesting.*

She poked her head into the library, wanting to wave goodbye to Bob. She could feel Davie's eyes on her. She gulped, then dared a glance. Her stomach flipped. She peered down at the ground, mumbling goodbyes. As she turned away, she could see Bob grinning and nodding his head suggestively, but Davie just glared at her, his jaw clamped down.

# Eleven

Davie was late. He was supposed to be helping Alfie with the farms fence repairs, but he didn't have the heart to leave Bob mid-game. They'd been playing chess every Thursday for the past ten years, since social services had shipped him there, just an angry teenager.

"Your go," prompted Bob. Davie moved his queen diagonally. He hadn't noticed the king on the next square.

Bob leaned back. "Are you kidding? You played right into my king there. Where is your flipping mind at today?"

His mind went to Maisy outside, talking to Logan. The way Maisy had flirtatiously swiped at him, and he'd whispered something into her ear. Logan's goal in life was to bed as many women as possible. The more temporary the woman, the better for him. Davie's ex – Logan's sister – used to joke about his many escapades tip-toeing from their house early in the morning. He hardly knew Maisy, and he couldn't offer her anything himself. He just really didn't want her to be another number-up for that creep.

The truth slipped out before he had time to think

about it. "I'm just a bit late. I told Alfie I'd help him on the farm."

"Then why are you sitting here with me? Get out there and help him."

\*\*\*

Davie hurried over to the field, full of apologies. Alfie had already started. The fence was looking more than a little wonky. As he pulled up, Alfie had a rope tied to the tractor and was attempting to pull out a tree that had fallen over the fencing. "Are ya flipping mad? That'll end up falling on your cab."

"How else am I supposed to pull it oot?"

"I'll get my chainsaw; we can chop it down, poison the roots after."

"Fine, fine," he murmured.

They circled the whole field, pulling out the broken fencing. Snapping it where they could, stacking it up on the tractor – one panel at a time until the whole lot was clear. Manual labour always gave him chance to digest anything bothering him, and Davie was feeling guilty for brushing Bob off. After all that man had given up for him, being a bit late wouldn't have hurt. But it was, what it was. He would be okay. He knew that much; Bob would always be okay.

Once they were happy that there was no fencing left, Davie hurried back to the shed to get his chainsaw. As he pulled open the huge wooden door, he glanced over the road. Maisy was sliding into the passenger seat of a metallic-blue BMW i4, her hair shiny with ringlets at the bottom, dressed in heels and jeans that hugged her hips and arse. He watched as Logan jumped into the driver's seat. He clenched his fists; he could just go over there and beat the shit out of the little office boy, but he'd be in the wrong. And where would that get him with Maisy?

"Fuck," he growled under his breath. He leaned his head on the wooden gate. He certainly hadn't been wrong about them flirting. With a bit of luck, maybe soon the woman would leave and stop interrupting everyone's lives. He dug the chainsaw out from under the pile of shovels and tools, knocking them flying. He didn't care; he stomped his way back across the field. He thought he heard Alfie say something about his face, but he wasn't sure. He sawed and banged and pulled until the entire tree was a pile of wood ready for the chipper. When he looked up and wiped the sweat from his brow, Alfie was watching him curiously.

"What?" snapped Davie.

Alfie shook his head. He walked over to his tractor, opened the door, and pulled two beers from a cooler bag, tossing one to Davie without a word. They sat on the tree trunk. Davie grunted in thanks, opened his can, and took a long swig.

After several minutes of silence, Alfie looked up at the side of Davie's face. "Everything alright, laddie?" he asked.

"Aye." Davie nodded.

"Now, you wanna tell me the truth?"

Davie peered around at him. Alfie had always been able to read him.

He sighed. "I don't think Bob needs Maisy. We're doing a perfectly decent job at looking after him and getting him his pain meds."

"What's it hurt to have a little help? She's here voluntarily."

"Outsiders come and upset the rhythm of things here and now it looks like she's dating Logan."

Alfie lifted his head and looked down at him. "And who might Logan be?"

"Hilda's grandson!"

"Oh, aye, Logan. And that's bad?"

"I just don't think she's here for the right reasons, and if that's the case, she'll make things worse for Bob."

Alfie took a swig of his beer then turned to look at Davie. "Make things worse for Bob? Or for you?" He leaned forward onto his elbows. "That Logan's certainly one for the ladies."

Davie could feel Alfie watching him. He smiled but he felt numb. Alfie wasn't stupid, but Davie didn't even know why it was pissing him off, he didn't want to be with another out-of-towner.

\*\*\*

When they were both tired and dirty, they decided to call it and day and made their way over to the Bull's Head for a pint of larger.

Alfie was hobbling out of the field and looked at him.

"What's up with ya?"

"Not as young as I used to be. All that pulling's made me stiff as a board."

"Ach. You'll out-live most of this village. You're a machine," Davie said with an affectionate smile.

"Pah!" Alfie pushed open the doors to the pub. A few

regulars stood around the bar chatting. A pop song played in the background. He spotted Grahame in fits of laughter as he talked to June Smith. Alfie made his way over to them, and Davie followed but as Jean stepped backwards, he saw a familiar messy bun of brown hair. Maisy was sat alone on a bar stool. She was spinning a coin, watching it, mesmerised. Then he saw her sway and watched her laugh at something Jack Cummings said. She was drunk. No one laughed at Jack's jokes, ever. He always smelt like stale clothes and made inappropriate jokes. If she was sober, he was positive that after five minutes with Jack Cummings she'd be tearing into him with that firecracker wit he'd seen.

Alfie had started talking to Grahame, he thought he heard him order drinks, but he couldn't take his eyes off Maisy. *What is she doing in here?* She lifted her drink above her head and hummed to herself. Davie felt his whole body go rigid. She'd been on a date with Logan. Is that why she was in there alone getting sloshed? Had Logan fucked her and chucked her?

Alfie followed Davie's eyes. He leaned his head in close and murmured, "Think someone started early on the juice."

He needed to get her out of that bar, but how? He approached her. "What did he do?" he growled, angrier than he'd expected.

Maisy jumped, then she scowled at him. "Hey, it's the sexy Viking!" she cheered sloppily.

"Viking? I thought you called me a hillbilly?"

"Only to your face."

"Maisy, did Logan hurt you?" he asked, his temperature rising.

"Logan?" she spluttered a little too loudly. "No! Not at all. How did you know I was even with him?"

"You're in Illvenie – everyone knows who you're with all of the time." *She's not going to like that*, he thought, knowing everyone knew her business. It might make her want to leave, but he needed her to understand.

She nodded, her lips pressed together in a thin line.

"If he didn't hurt you, then what's this?" He nodded toward the vodka glass she was sloshing around in her hand.

"Just fancied a drink. It has been a weird sort of a day. None of your business really, is it?"

He sat on the stool next to her. "Well, no, but it's a cycle. I know about cycles. You need to stop before it evolves. Pah! Nee mind, you won't listen anyway. People like you nee do."

For a moment she stared at him, a scowl on her face. He scowled back. Why was he so angry? Why was he worried about her? She wasn't his problem. He faltered. "Sorry. I didn't mean anything by it."

"What are you going on about?"

"I mean you shouldn't drink when you feel down."

"What makes you think I feel down? I'm happy," she cried, sloshing her glass in the air again.

"Maisy," he growled. "Please can I take you home?"

"Ooh, is that an offer?"

"Maisy?" He pleaded this time.

"Fine. I'm ready to go, anyway. You can walk me if you like."

She got up. Davie caught her as she was about to trip. She gave him a flirtatious smile as he put his hand on her hip. It was driving him crazy. She knew she was attractive, and she was toying with him because she was drunk. He nodded to Alfie as he walked outside.

As they walked down the road, he couldn't help but laugh as she swayed along, singing to herself.

She stopped in the middle of the road and put her hands on her hips. "What are you laughing at?" she demanded.

"Nothing." He sighed. "Come on, let's get you back," he said, dragging her along. "So, are you going to tell me what he did to upset you yet?" he asked.

"He didn't do anything, honest. It was a crap date. I didn't like him. It's weird, I've always fancied arrogant alpha men in suits, not men like you!" she slurred.

He smirked at that. "Oh really?"

She beamed up at him and nodded. He wanted her to elaborate but prodding her for more information whilst drunk would have felt like reading a woman's diary. You just don't do it.

"So, what did upset you then?"

"I'm fine, Davie!"

"So, you always get drunk alone, do you?"

"No. Ugh." She sighed loudly. "If you must know, I don't think I can help Bob. It's all a big waste of time. And I can't sleep in that house; its freezing and there's a lion waiting to eat me."

*So, it really isn't anything to do with Logan. Wait, did she say lion?*

"There are no lions around here, lass."

She stopped walking again and looked at him. "I heard it with my own ears."

"You're just drunk."

"Not now! Last night when it was prowling around outside my door."

"What makes you think it was a lion?"

"It sounded like one."

"How?"

"How?" she asked.

"Yeah, how did it sound like a lion?"

For a moment she fell silent, and he wondered if she'd given up trying to convince him. But suddenly, she opened her mouth wide and growled into the night air. Davie burst into laughter.

"Oh aye? Maybe it was Alfie passing by after a pint or two." He sniggered.

Her face was serious. "No, it was all night. Like a kind of a... *raow* sound. More like *roaw*." She attempted the noise again and Davie's laugh snorted out of his nose.

"Stop laughing at me!" she demanded.

"Sorry, but that's a good impression. The animal you're hearing is a deer," he said, still grinning.

"Deer? They do not make that noise!"

"Ever heard one?"

He watched her contemplating the question, a finger on her chin. Then she peered back at him, and he watched her shiver. "No, but that can't be right."

"Aye, it's a dear alright," he said simply. "Ask anyone around here."

He took off his coat and put it over her shoulders as they meandered down the hill. He looked down at the wellington boots on her feet.

"Good to see you in more suitable footwear."

"You like them? They're from the farm."

"Aye, left insole missing too?"

She turned and looked at him in surprise. "You really do know everything around here." She laughed.

He smiled back at her. "They were mine when I was aboot fifteen. Bob never throws any good boots away."

"They're comfy," she said, smiling.

"I'm sorry that your date was a bit shite, Mais," he mused.

She grinned at him. "No, you're not."

"No, I'm not," he said, smirking.

"Well, it wasn't a complete fail. There are some nice restaurants in Inverness. It's the first time I've ever been."

"Are there?" he replied.

"You've never been?" she asked, looking at him in surprise.

"Only for groceries, prescriptions, or the odd pair of boots."

"Oh. You should try it. I suppose it is a little expensive though." He watched her for a moment as she looked out at the night sky, clouds of white air expelling from her mouth. She must have thought he was broke. He didn't care. He wasn't a money man, but it was the assumption. He couldn't possibly have money, because he didn't wear it on his sleeve; it was presumptions and shallow.

"This coat's really warm." She sighed, snuggling in.

"Aye and it's not Joe Blogs or whatever the kids wear these days either."

She giggled at that.

"It's lasted me five years and it's still good as new. Designed to keep you warm in down to minus-twenty degrees!"

"Minus-twenty degrees! How cold does it get in Scotland?"

"Not that cold. Don't worry."

"I can't imagine having a coat for five years. I don't think any of mine have lasted more than six months."

"Shocker." He said, sighing.

"Oh c'mon. I can see the judgment in your eyes."

"You and I, Maisy, are from two different worlds."

They reached Corinuck, and she started to shrug the coat off, he put his hand on her arm.

"Keep it. See if it helps you during the night."

She glanced at his hand on her arm, and he removed it awkwardly. She looked up at him though her lashes. "Davie? Will you stop with me tonight? Protect me from the deer lion?"

He gulped. He'd like nothing more than to spend the night with her. Even if it was just to hold her whilst she slept. He gulped down the lump in his throat and looked into her eyes. Bands of nerves pooled in his stomach. "I don't think that's a good idea." His breath hitched. He watched the look of annoyance pass over her face.

"Fine. I won't offer again," she said, gulping. He didn't know what to say. For several moments they both stood in silence. Maisy wobbled on her boots. She started tugging at the shoulder of his coat again.

"If you're going to walk back to the Bull, then you should definitely take your coat with you. You'll get cold," she said.

He put a hand on top of hers to stop her from pulling it off. "I'll survive." He never wanted to take his hand from hers. "And besides, maybe I'll take a trip into Inverness soon and buy another one."

She rocked back on her heels; she too left her hand where it was. "Maybe you should take me. I can help you find one." Her pupils momentarily dilated. He imagined grabbing the collar of his coat and pulling her in, pressing his lips to hers. But she was tipsy, and also, leaving, he reminded himself, and as irritating as hell. What was he thinking? He removed his hand, the thought instantly sobering him. He was suddenly very aware of his hand hanging limp by his side, feeling cold and numb. He didn't know how to respond to her question. Shopping? Together?

"You've got to be kidding!" he spluttered.

She looked offended. "But I could help you choose something that would suit you!"

"My point exactly," he said, backing away and laughing.

"What? I'm great at picking out clothes. Ask anyone," she called into the night.

Davie chuckled to himself as he walked away, heading up the hill. His heart was pounding like he'd just ran a damn marathon. The woman was twisting him up like a matted ram.

# Twelve

Maisy woke with a start, the face of a lion prowling around in the dark at the forefront of her mind. She looked at her phone – it was 3am. She closed her eyes, but it wasn't working. It was cold, and she could hear the noises of the night again. She drank some water, went to the toilet, and paced back and forth listening carefully, trying to work out the distance between the house and the sounds. Then she heard something like screams in the distance. She grabbed Davie's coat from the chair, jumped back into bed and tucked herself inside, tented from the outside world. The smell engulfed her, a mixture of cut grass, wood, and just a hint of a musky aftershave that she had never smelt before Illvenie. Before she'd stood in close proximity to *him*, the day she'd walked into Corinuck.

She breathed it in, letting it warm and soothe her body until the sounds drifted away. She pictured Davie standing outside, the look on his face when she'd asked him to stay. He'd looked scared. Had she read the signals wrong? She closed her eyes tight, felt herself melt into the fabric padding, remembering the image of him laughing, a soft glint in his eye. The same way he'd looked at her when she'd stood in cow dung. Had she mistakenly seen it as admiration?

\*\*\*

Maisy emptied the kettle, watching the flakes of limescale as they dropped into the sink. She refilled it, turning on the huge clunky tap. Turning around she was startled to find Hilda standing beside her. She was dressed in a purple kimono with red coral clogs on her feet; the woman had a boho hippy style that was one on its own.

"I hear you and Logan had a nice time last night?" Hilda said with a wiggle of her eyebrows.

Maisy smiled at her awkwardly. She didn't want to give the poor woman the wrong impression. "Yes, it was nice thanks, Hilda. It's always good to make new friends, in new places."

Hilda placed her wrinkled hands flat on the kitchen work surface, her bracelets rattling. "I see," she said with a wink. "If he asks, I'll tell him you're not on the lookout. Us girls got to stick together."

Maisy smiled at her. She took two cups of tea to the library and placed one down in front of Bob. "How are you today?"

"Bloody great." He grimaced.

"Not so good?"

"I've been worse since your visit on Monday."

Maisy's shoulders deflated. "I'm sorry, Bob."

"Oh, I wasn't blaming you, love. I didn't mean…" he tailed off.

"I know." She nodded. "Sometimes, getting things moving again hurts. But after a while, that pain goes away, and that's when the magic happens. Would you like to do some stretches today?"

He pursed his upper lip.

"It might help," she encouraged.

"Alright, but not too much."

She began manipulating and massaging his calves the way the Angie had shown her. Bob seemed to relax a little.

"I hope you're taking care of that laddie of ours. He might seem tough as a bull, but his heart is as tender as yours or mine."

*Hilda must have told everyone*, she thought. "Oh, Bob, it was just dinner. We're just friends," she said, slathering more strong-smelling oil onto her gloved hands and working her way down to his ankles.

"Not Logan!" He guffawed. "Oh no! I knew that wouldn't go anywhere. You're too good for him!"

She laughed. "Oh, am I now? How do you know that?"

"He's a ladies' man, that one. Not for you. Davie is the one for you. And you like him, I can see it."

She rolled her chair closer to his, squirting oil onto his hands and rubbing it between his fingers. She looked up at him and smiled.

"He likes you too, you know," he said. "He's a much better fit. But don't tell Hilda I said that, or she'll be after my head," he whispered.

"It's our secret. But don't get your hopes up, Bob. It's not like that between us." She sat up, pulled off her gloves, and tossed them into the bin. "Now, would you like to go for a walk in the garden?"

He smirked as though he knew better. Old men always thought they knew better.

"I canee make it to the garden on these useless bloody things." He smacked his legs.

"How about I take you in the chair and you try a couple of steps on the grass?"

"I don't know, it's pretty bumpy on the grass."

"For me? Please!" she pleaded.

He looked at her and blew out air between his lips.

"Alright, but you better catch me if I fall."

"I will!"

"Can't resist a pretty lady me, that's my trouble. Always was."

She laughed as she went to the hall to fetch his chair.

"And if I walk for you, will you give our Davie a try?" Bob asked.

"Oh, be off with ya." She laughed, pushing his chair outside.

\*\*\*

Eventually, Maisy got Bob to try a couple of steps. He smiled the whole time, despite the underlying grimace. Then he slumped into his chair and looked around at the garden. Maisy looked at him, concerned.

"Are you in pain, Bob?"

"No more than usual. No point whining like a wee bairn though, aye."

She gave him a sideway glance, grinning, then looked out over the rolling fields. "This view is spectacular." She sighed.

"Aye, it's a nice walk over those fields on a mild day too. Carey loved it out here. She spent a lot of time making this garden pretty. She liked to sit out on a nice day and have breakfast amongst the flowers. Nothing like orange juice and bacon in the sunshine, the smell of flowers in the warm breeze. That is until you get swarmed in bees, and you have to pack it all away in a hurry." He smirked, rubbing his chin. "She would have hated to see it like this, you know. It's as though it's lost its magic, all overgrown and ugly. Much like everything else when she's not around, I suppose."

"Carey sounds like a good woman."

"She was a hell of a woman!"

"How long were you together?"

"Fifty-one years," he said proudly.

"Wow! How did you meet?"

"She was a rookie in the media. A trainee. They sent her to my farm, to interview me about an infestation of bugs that was killing local crops. She was a terrible interviewer; she got no info at all." He laughed at the memory. Maisy smiled. "I was worried she would get the sack. So, I asked if she wanted to get a bite to eat at the Bull, said I'd give her all the details she needed. I may have been influenced by her beauty, of course. But, to my dissatisfaction, she was totally professional. I tried to pursue her after that; she'd go out on a date with me then say she was too busy. She didn't want to get into a relationship whilst she was trying to begin her career, you see. So, I became her friend. Listened to her woes, travelled forty miles to take her dinner and wine when she was exhausted. And we'd sit together, either in total silence or chatting all night long. Some nights we didn't sleep for talking."

"Oh yeah, is that what you call it," she jibed.

"Aye, there was none of that funny business. We went on like that, just talking, for over two years. Then one day, she met someone else."

"Oh no!" Maisy gasped.

"Yep, she told me over the phone that she'd met someone. Said she was going out on a date with him the next evening. That was when I realised that I loved her. I drove to her house, asked her out for cake."

"Cake?"

"Yeah, I knew she had a weakness for yellow sponge cake, so she couldn't say no. I had the bakery staff sneak a ring into the sponge for me. And I proposed, there and then. We hadn't even kissed before that day. She thought I was insane. All that time, she'd assumed I wasn't interested and had given up hope. She'd liked me all along and I didn't see it. She said yes, of course. And we never looked back, even when we were at our worst."

"How did you know she wouldn't say no to your proposal?"

His eyes widened. "I didn't. I was bloody terrified. But I'd rather have been rejected by her than pursued by anybody else, any day."

Maisy squeezed her hand over her heart. "Aww."

"What can I say? When you know, you know," he said.

She turned and looked over the garden. "We could get her garden back. Surely, we could."

"No point." He sighed. "It won't be the same without her, it will probably just make it more obvious that she's not around to enjoy it."

"Or it will be somewhere you can go to enjoy the memories of her."

"It's been left too long. It wouldn't look the same."

"I bet if we trimmed down all of this long stuff, you'd see the old shapes beneath."

"Who's gonna do it, anyway? I won't be of much use to you, will I?" He chuckled.

"What if I asked Davie to help me? You could give us instructions."

"Davie hates being told what to do."

"I'm sure he can take instruction." She sighed.

He looked at her. "Yes, but he's got enough to contend with on the farm. The past is the past." He sighed. They sat in silence, hands gripped around mugs of tea, looking around, and she wondered if they were both picturing it, his image from the past, hers from the future.

"He was the apple of Carey's eye, you know."

"Davie?"

"Of course, Davie."

"He told me he sees you as a father figure."

"I should think so too. We were basically his parents."

She looked at him in surprise.

"He didn't tell you?" She shook her head. "Davie lived with us from the age of nine." He paused; his eyes glazed over as he spoke. She wondered if he was thinking out loud rather than sharing the story, but she kept quiet all the same. "The moment my sister overdosed, Carey took the reins with Davie. I've got to be honest; I wasn't so sure we'd cope with a young man in the house. He was my nephew, aye, but I barely knew the kid and he seemed like a problem to me. But Carey. Wooo." He blew out. "She was good with bairns; she knew she could love him back to earth and that's exactly what she did. It doesn't always work, of course, but she saw something in him."

"Davie was a problem child?" she asked, wondering if Bob's memory was what it should be. He looked startled, as though he'd forgotten she was there, and then he continued with a warm smile.

"Oh aye! He's no trouble now, hasn't been for many years. But back then, he was troubled. Starting fires, getting into fights… phew, he had hassle following him everywhere, that lad. Still, it wasn't the bairn's fault. He'd seen his mum run from one addiction to another in Glasgow. And he was fighting everyone along the way in honour of the woman. Poor thing."

The Davie she'd met seemed so calm and in control. He seemed as though he'd always been here, living this old-fashioned way of life and yet, once he'd lived in Glasgow getting into fights? Was that why he hated seeing her a little drunk? It reminded him of his mum…

"You must both miss her."

"Yep. She'd have done anything for our Davie. She'd have liked you too."

"If you don't mind me asking, how did she die?"

"Sepsis. It came from a water infection. Unfortunately, we left it too long for her to get the antibiotics into her system."

Her mouth gaped open and she turned to look at him sideways. She remembered Davie walking out of the shop when she'd suggested people would get sepsis if they didn't find a better system.

"Wait, so she died because she couldn't get the prescription in time?"

Had Davie blamed himself? Had her words cemented that for him?

"Not really. At first, we thought it would go away on it's own. We were busy on the farm." He smiled fondly. "Then she took really ill, and it was hard getting her to the doctors in Inverness. And then they couldn't get her an appointment due to the lockdown. Then she finally got a prescription, but the infection wasn't shifting." She noticed his eyes darting around, his chest rising and falling heavier. "She had several prescriptions. I thought she was improving. Then we were in the kitchen here, plucking a chicken, and she just collapsed. It took us two hours to get to A&E. By then, it was too late."

"Wow... I can't imagine."

He shook his head. "No, it's not good to think about either..."

"Does it make living here difficult for you?"

"The memories?"

"No. I mean having no local hospital close by to help when she was in need. Do you blame yourself? Do you worry that it could happen to you or Davie?"

He took in a deep breath. "I don't look at it like that. Living here gave us life. What other option is there? Live out there..." He looked out into the distance. "In a world where all people care about is money? We have a community here. We care for one another. Carey lived a fulfilled life. She was an old-fashioned woman at heart, and here she got to create this beautiful garden, bake cakes for our neighbours and friends and ride her beloved horses." He shook his head. "No, she wouldn't have been happy anywhere else, and neither would we. Then you're talking quality of life versus time on the planet. She was a content woman – I wouldn't jeopardise that for all the time in the world."

"That's weird to hear. Most people will do anything to preserve their lives or the lives of the people they love. I never looked at it like that."

"And you don't think it's selfish?"

"I'm not sure. I could ask you the same question," she responded, rubbing her knuckles into the palm of her hand.

They sat in silence for a few minutes, Maisy scouring her brain for questions to ask. She'd got too caught up in his stories and forgotten what she was trying to achieve.

"You had horses?" she asked, attempting to lighten the mood.

He grimaced. "Oh yes, still do. I have some photos around here if you want to see?"

"I'd love to."

He wheeled into the kitchen and came back a few moments later, a box overflowing with photos toppling from his knee. He started rifling through them, passing her his favourites, dropping a few and explaining each one. "She taught a few of the local bairns when they were young," he told her.

"Davie too?"

"Aye, mucking-out and riding seemed to calm him. Then, of course, he used to help me too. We had cows, sheep, chickens. The three of us worked hard, but we also had a lot of good times. Look." He passed her a photo; it was Davie milking a cow, the milk spraying into the air, Carey running to the rescue, a smile on her face.

Maisy smiled warmly. "Looks like you both gave him a magical childhood."

"At times, it felt it. It wasn't without its struggles, but we wouldn't have wanted it any other way. I just wish she'd been able to experience kids of her own. Or at least grandbabies. Davie's got to get married someday. She'd have loved that. Yeah, I'd rather die here where part of her still exists to me, than ever live in a neighbourhood where people turn their backs on one another for a wee quid."

As she pushed his wheelchair inside, she contemplated his words. She'd seen plenty of online inspirational quotes about life being the real poverty, but it had passed her by. Until now, something had her thinking. Could true happiness really be achievable without money? Money was the one thing that got you places, opportunities, even acceptance. Was it possible she was looking at it all wrong?

# Thirteen

Davie flipped the spade, dropping loose mud onto the solid pile. He had to hand it to the girl, she'd been there all day, pulling weeds and trimming bushes alongside him. Just like she'd promised. They had Bob sitting in his wheelchair with a cup of tea and a blanket over his legs, watching them, telling them stories about the past. Davie hadn't heard him speak about Carey in a couple of years; it warmed him to hear it all again as a fond memory instead of a painful reminder. He was always surprised by how much he had in common with Carey; after all, she wasn't his biological mother.

He watched Maisy's face intently as she listened with genuine interest.

"So, when she planted the begonia's, Davie and I had been out birthing a baby calf; it was his first time. Davie was so excited to come and tell her about it, he came running out the back as fast as his legs would carry him. The thing was, he didn't realise that the patio doors were closed. And, of course, he smacked straight into the glass. Almost knocked himself out. Carey was worried sick.

When he went to sleep that night, she just sat by his side watching the rise and fall of his chest. Making sure he was still breathing." He chuckled. "I swear she didn't sleep a wink that night."

He watched Maisy gasp and cover her mouth with her hand as though to stop herself from laughing.

In the centre of the garden, Davie tackled a patch of weeds as tall as him. "Look at this!" he called back to Maisy and Bob.

Maisy stomped through the long grass, she stood beside him, and peeped in between the weeds. "That looks interesting."

He looked at her. "I don't remember it."

"Let's fix it up. Maybe then you will!" she said. She was so close he could smell her familiar perfume, all citrus and musk. They both stared at the tall-standing bird table in wonder.

"Do you think its home-made?" Maisy asked in a whisper. He turned to look at her, her close eye contact overwhelmed him enough to deem him wordless.

"Carey made that herself," came Bob's voice. They both turned around. Bob was standing right behind them, looking in, his face close to theirs. Davie and Maisy looked at Bob and then down at his legs. Maisy was looking back at him open-mouthed.

"It's beautiful." Maisy said, exhaling loudly. "The bird table. It's beautiful," she repeated.

Davie gulped; a buzz bolted from his toes to his core. *She is beautiful.*

Bob coughed. Davie put a supportive hand under his elbow and led him back to his wheelchair. "I can't believe you've just walked by yourself. How long have you been able to do that? It's been forever since I saw you walk."

"It's nice watching you two work as a team on the garden," he murmured and Davie wondered if he hadn't heard his question or if he had simply chosen to evade it. "Carey and I used to pull weeds together you know. I'm not a spiritual person but I believe it bonded our souls, all of that, being at one with the earth."

Maisy raised her eyebrows at him and smirked. Davie felt himself blush. He had no idea how to stop Bob from talking. Aside from letting go of his wheelchair on top of the hill, of course. He chuckled to himself as he imagined it, but immediately regretted such twisty thoughts, he loved Bob.

\*\*\*

As the afternoon wore on, they finally made a clearing within a mudded area that was cornered off by blue-patterned concrete. Davie was turning the soil, ignoring the buzzing of his phone from his pocket. It had been ringing on and off all afternoon. He knew Alfie would want his help, and he was supposed to look at June's gasket on her Fiesta at 2pm. He knew he didn't have time to complete this project. But when Maisy had asked him, he'd been incapable of saying no. He pulled his phone from his pocket.

Maisy started laughing. "What on earth is that?" She chuckled through her open hand.

"What do you mean? It's my phone."

He knew exactly what she meant. He'd had the damn thing for almost six years. She stood up and walked over. "It looks like something from the '90s!"

He covered his phone. "Shhh, you'll offend her."

"Oh, it's a *she* now, is it? Doesn't have a name, does it?"

"Sammy. Sammy Samsung."

She leant back and laughed. Davie wondered if he'd ever heard anything sound so sweet.

"Hey, stranger."

They both turned to the sound of the voice. Davie felt an immediate irritation.

"Hey, Logan," replied Maisy, grinning enthusiastically.

*Logan. Even his name sounds annoying and obnoxious.* Davie nodded at him, his lips remained tight. He didn't want to be rude. Of course, he also didn't want to be welcoming.

"Maisy. Davie," Logan replied in a clipped tone.

Davie thought he heard the guy's voice dip when he'd said his name, but he wasn't sure. Logan walked straight over to Maisy and pulled her in for a hug. They stood close, facing each other, chatting. It looked intimate. Davie patted the mud around his first planted begonia, then stood back and looked at it proudly.

His head buzzed; he was trying not to listen to their conversation, but he couldn't help himself.

"I haven't been in to see Hilda yet today. How is she?" Maisy asked.

Logan lowered his head and murmured as though embarrassed. "I must confess, I've not seen her yet. I heard you were here and couldn't wait to say hello to you first."

"Oh," she said and grinned.

*Barf.* Davie grabbed his spade and turned around. And there was JD pissing all over his begonia. He stood up straight and watched as the dog marched off, head and tail pointed to the sky. *I'd bet Logan taught it to do that.* He smiled and shook his head at his own stupidity.

"Maisy, would you mind if we went in now?" croaked Bob. "I think I've had enough action for one day." He gave her one of his feeblest of looks and Davie eyed him suspiciously.

"Of course!" Maisy turned away from Logan.

"Sorry, Logan. Hope you don't mind me stealing her from you?" Bob said, adding more strain into his voice.

Logan smiled. "Of course not."

Bob glanced up at Davie and winked. Davie tried not to laugh; he shook his head in disbelief.

"Catch up with you later, Logan," Maisy called back, making her way inside with the wheelchair.

"Aye," he said, looking around disappointed. "I need to go and see Hilda anyway." He followed her in, and when they walked into the kitchen, Logan turned right. But Davie couldn't help but watch Logan as he watched Maisy walking away. He clenched his fists, turned around and continued to stab the spade in the ground and turn over the soil.

\*\*\*

Maisy came back out twenty minutes later, followed by Logan. "Sorry, maybe another time," she was saying, smiling her winning smile at him.

"Aye, definitely," Logan commented, his eyes darting to Davie and back again.

"Okay, well, it was good to see you," she said, gesturing at the garden.

He walked back inside, looking slightly dismayed. She seemed not to notice.

Davie had cleared the area with the bird table completely. Maisy stood next to him. "It looks great." She said with a smile.

He looked around. "I can really see it all coming along. Thank you, Maisy."

She turned to look at him. "For what? You did the majority of the work."

He looked at the toes of his shoes and rocked back on his heels. "We did it together. But I wasn't thanking you for that."

She raised her eyebrows at him.

"Her garden meant so much to her, and it was here all along. Despite that, it never crossed my mind to do this, until you came wading in with that persuasive bluntness of yours. Now it's like I can feel her presence here again. And Bob feels it too, I can see fragments of the man I admired growing up, starting to show again."

She put her hand on his arm and leaned into him. "It must have been hard losing the woman you knew as your mum."

He nodded and looked down at her.

"Well, I, for one, am knackered. You, on the other hand, look like you could still go another ten rounds. Can I have some of what you're on?" He chuckled.

She leaned back and laughed. "Looks can be deceiving. I'm about ready for bed."

He cocked his eyebrow as though she was being suggestive. Her eyes widened before she smacked him, grinning playfully.

He smiled back indulgently. "Fancy a beer?" he asked.

She sat down on the grass and pursed her lips. "Why not?"

He went inside and took two bottles of beer from the fridge. "Alfie's been in here looking for you," said Bob.

"Oh aye?"

"I told him you'd help him finish up tomorrow."

"Was he not annoyed?"

"Don't worry, I told him I wouldn't let you go till you'd finished my job."

"Thanks, Bob." He smiled, making his way back out into the garden. Maisy was looking out over the fields thoughtfully. Davie sat down next to her and passed her a bottle of beer.

"You looked surprised at me having beer. I have a stash here for when we have late nights with Bob."

"It's not that. I thought you frowned upon drinking."

"What makes you think that?" he asked, lifting his cap at the peak.

"The night you found me drunk in the Bull, you looked upset."

His mouth tightened and he looked at the ground between his feet. "I wasn't upset with *you*, Maisy." His voice was gruff. "There's having a beer and then there's drinking beyond your capability. The two things are entirely different. It worries me to see people crossing that boundary, especially people I care about."

She chewed her bottom lip. "Because of your mum?" she asked, her voice soft and quiet.

His eyes pierced into hers. "I might have known." He looked to the sky. "You can't keep anything to yourself around here." He started straight into her eyes then. "Yes, because of my mum," Davie said into a sigh.

"Sorry," Maisy whispered. "I didn't mean to be in your business."

He felt her apology settle somewhere behind his ribs. "It's okay." He released lungs-full of air. "I suppose I'm used to people knowing my business."

They sat in silence for a moment, but he didn't feel like he needed to make a joke or say the first thing that came to mind like he normally would in company. He looked at her; she took a swig of beer straight from the bottle. She had her jeans rolled up to her ankles and her previously clean, smart, white blouse was tied in a knot around her waist, only at that point, it was splatted with mud. Her eyelashes were a normal length now, and her nails were cut down to the quick with dirt under them. The first moment he'd seen her clambering from the hedge of Willie's trail, he hadn't thought she could get any more beautiful, and yet, she had. She was naturally stunning.

He took the cap from his own head and pushed it onto her head, over her ponytail, then appraised her.

"There. You really look the part now."

She grinned at him. "The part?"

"You know. What d'ya call it? The hillbilly part." He grinned. "Only sexier than any country girl I've ever met."

She laughed and glanced down at herself. "I don't feel sexy."

He turned to her and spoke in a low voice. "That's because you don't see you through my eyes. Oh, wait, does the sexy bit make you a Viking?"

"Ha-ha, very funny. I don't think Vikings are sexy. I just said that you looked like a sexy Viking when you're actually a bit of a hillbilly."

"I'll take that." He smirked.

Maisy turned back to the field, grinning into the open mouth of her beer bottle. "You're a good man, Davie. Look at what you're doing here for a start… After all you've been through. I could only wish to be as kind-hearted as you. I just don't think about other people."

He pushed his hand through his hair, trying to work out if he'd heard her right. "It's like you're blind. I cannee understand, how you never see how fucking amazing you are."

She turned away then, looking embarrassed. She took another swig from her bottle, and looked up at the sky. He watched her put a hand on her diaphragm and he heard her inhale. It reminded him again of the first time he saw her.

"What *is* that?" he asked.

"What's what?"

"That thing you do, with the hand and the breathing." He mimicked her movement and she grinned.

"It's a practice called Buteyako. It's said to be calming."

Davie swept back his hair and wiggled his nose. "You're in the calmest place on earth right now. This view is therapy alone, you don't need Butt yakee or whatever it is."

"Butt yakee?" She laughed.

"Aye, it comes from a *coorie nook*," he said, side-eyeing her.

She laughed. "Bute-eee-yako." She sounded it out.

"Yes, that. Anyhow… not required out here. The

calmest place on earth. In fact, lets rename it Illvie-yakee."

"Like karaoke?" She smiled, leaning forward to rest her elbows onto her knees. "Illvie-yakee, I am most agreeable. However, I wasn't trying to find calm just then."

"Oh, you weren't?"

"Nope. I was consuming the energy and storing it for when I go home. It's just so damn peaceful – the place, the company, the stars. This is one for my bank of calm."

"Oh, aye, makes total fucking sense," Davie said sarcastically, chuckling to himself. She leaned to the side and nudged him, he didn't budge. He got a waft of that warm citrus smell of hers and he inhaled. "Although, I've got to agree with you," he continued, "you can't beat the fucking company."

They grinned at each other. The fact that she was enjoying his company made him smile from the inside out. But what did it mean? Was she attracted to him? He couldn't overthink it. She clearly only wanted a friendship with him, she was temporary. He lowered his head. And what about Logan? Did she feel at peace with him too? He wanted to ask, he was trying to decide how to, when she stood up.

"I should get back now. Take a warm bath to defrost my bones."

Davie stood up with her. "Oh, aye, yes, we've been out here all day, and the temperature has dropped a fair bit. You must be getting stiff as a board now." He tried not to think about her in the bath defrosting, otherwise she wouldn't be the only one getting stiff as a board.

"I'm good," she replied, sweeping grass from the back of her trousers. She straightened up and glared at him, her huge eyes landing on his. Jesus Christ, his body was sending signals in all directions. He stared back at her, unable to move. "Maybe now I will actually sleep tonight."

He stretched and pushed his hands through his hair. "Do you want me to sit outside ya door tonight? Make sure no tigers come around to eat you in the night?" He sniggered.

"Nope. I've made it for the last eleven nights; I'm sure I won't be eaten tonight."

"Then the least I can do is walk you back to the hoose."

"You don't need…"

"I want to."

They walked the lane in a comfortable silence. He couldn't get her words out of his mind. She felt at peace with him. Was he reading into a passing comment or was she feeling what he was feeling. He gulped.

"What would you do if you were offered a permanent position here? Would you stay?"

"I don't think so. I still haven't found my calling, not really. And it's just not normality for me." She tugged at a strand of hair and veered her eyes to it. "My roots are starting to grow, my nails look terrible, and all of my lashes fell out within days. I don't think I could live like that long term."

He rubbed a hand over his beard and tittered. "Jesus Christ. Maisy."

"What?" she said, giggling.

He kicked at the dusty stones. "The first time I saw you, coming out of Willie's trail with your make-up all done, hair askew, long lashes, nails with those weird jewels – I thought, that's one beautiful woman."

"You could have fooled me; you couldn't get away fast enough. And when I spoke to you, you seemed irritated by me. Not the normal reaction I get from men." She smiled and nudged him again.

"I didn't say I was smart." Davie grimaced.

"You're different, but that's one of the things I like about you."

"Oh aye?" he said with a grin.

She smirked up at him.

"Anyway, as I was saying, you looked fooking beautiful. But now, now without all of that make-up and pampering… you look fooking terrible."

"What?" she gasped, turning to face him.

He laughed. "I'm kidding, I'm kidding. Naw, what I was saying was that now I can't take my fooking eyes off of you. You're breathtaking, Maisy; I have to keep pinching myself that you're real and not a fantasy created in my own mind."

"You're teasing me again." She groaned.

"Naw, I'm serious, lass. I think this look suits you, perfectly. The soft peachy skin, working hands, the dirty shirt. Even my hat looks better on you than it ever did me." His mouth was drying up.

She laughed. "Well, thank you. My friends and family would shit if they saw me like this."

"They'd shit?" he asked, chuckling.

"Midlands slang." She scoffed.

He nodded and smiled. "I'll have to take your word for that."

They stepped off the road onto the gravel. "So, your friends and family would 'shit', aye? But how aboot you?"

She raised her eyebrows. "I do feel strangely relaxed like this, but that worries me."

He tilted his head at her, raising one eyebrow as he ambled along. "I think you just like to worry."

"No, but what if I get ugly. What if, it's so gradual that I don't even notice? I can't just let go of myself like that."

"Beauty is subjective."

"Beauty is marketing, backed by popular belief. But you need it to get anywhere in life."

"Rubbish! That's misguided. Look at me! I'm killing it out here in the stables. All the cows love me. Maybe you're just choosing the wrong company."

He was walking slower now, enjoying their conversation. She was following his lead, kicking at the stones. *I'd rather speak crap to her all day than talk to anyone else*, he thought.

Maisy snorted. "Are you saying I should choose animals over people?"

"There are many different circles of people in this world, Maisy. Even I know that, and I live in seclusion."

"I suppose. But I did always prefer animals, so I could probably roll with that," she said, grinning.

"We have more in common than you think," he said with a laugh. "Either way, you couldn't be ugly if you tried!"

"Well, thanks… I think." She laughed. "But you don't get it! How could you?"

Something hooted in the background. He turned to look at her, she barley flinched.

"I'm both impressed and a little disappointed," Davie said, grinning.

"Eh?"

"The noises of the night, you barely even noticed."

"It was just an owl, Davie!" Maisy said, rolling her eyes.

"Exactly. But only a week ago you'd have jumped into my arms at that wee sound."

"No, I wouldn't!" she said, laughing.

But they both knew she would have. She was adjusting, and it disturbed him how much he liked that fact.

"So, tell me, what would change in your life if you stayed natural?"

"Ugh, I'm so bored of this conversation now. Tell me something about you, please. You never wanted to move anywhere else, somewhere busier?"

He was pushing her, and he wasn't sure why... did he want her to stay? The last thing he wanted to do was try and convince her of that. He couldn't stand the rejection all over again, and what if she was just being polite to him.

"Na, I don't need to go anywhere. I've got my own lashes, nails, and hair. All natural as well." He put his fingers under his chin and pouted.

"Not for that..." She giggled. "I just mean – you'd never want to move anywhere else. Like, away from here?"

"I've no reason to be anywhere else; I'm happy here. And besides, I have people relying on me. I could never leave them."

"Must be the honourable hillbilly in you." She laughed; he chuckled back.

"Yeah, like the towny in you. We're two different people, eh?" He felt the mood flatten. They *were* two different people. They crossed the field in silence, hearing only the whistles of the wind, one streetlight barely lighting their way.

He couldn't help turning to look at her as they walked. How much she'd changed on the outside. And still, everything about her sparkled. She brought life to the old village. She was a year younger than him, yet even her skin seemed to be bursting with youth. It was like he was missing her already and she hadn't left yet. He suddenly couldn't imagine being there without her. He didn't want to be there without her, he realised.

She turned and caught his eye.

"What?" she asked shyly.

"I just canee get over how beautiful you are," he heard himself say.

She stopped and looked at him, her eyes glistened in the night. He followed his instinct and leaned into her. He placed his lips gently on hers; they felt warm and soft. She opened his mouth with her tongue slowly and leaned in closer, deepening the kiss. They clashed together. Hastily, her hands running through his hair, gently tugging at the roots. His hand was running up the soft skin of her neck. As the kiss deepened further, their movements became more frantic. Their breaths became louder. His hand gripped the side of her waist. She groaned. The sound caused a tightening in his pants.

"Fuck," he murmured into her mouth. She ran her hands down his back, grabbing tightly around his arse cheek.

"Oh, I wouldn't do that." He growled the words harsher than he meant and heard her breath hitch, felt her groin pressed into his and then she pulled away, panting. He felt the need to grab himself, he ached so bad. "What are you doing to me?" he asked, stretching the groin of his jeans away from himself.

"Davie. We shouldn't be doing this." She gasped.

"Is it Logan?"

Her eyes widened. "No! There's nothing between me and him!" she yelled.

"You should try telling him that!"

His boner was gone.

"Look, forget Logan," she said. "Davie, I'm only here for another six weeks. My time in this position is almost up."

"Then we should make the most of today!"

"Then what? Do you really think it's wise to start something and then walk away?"

"Well, you went on a date with Logan. Where did you see that going?"

She backed away. "Ugh," she shrieked. "Go home, Davie, will you, you're getting on my nerves."

"You know what? I don't understand bloody woman. All up and down all the time."

"Have you ever considered it might not be women, but you? You don't bloody listen."

"And yer noot listening to me!"

"Ugh," she screamed again. She walked inside and shut the door on him.

He stomped up the hill. Feeling frustrated, annoyed, and ravenous, he needed a cold shower. "Pain in the arse," he muttered to himself.

# Fourteen

Maisy closed the door. She leant against it and sank down to the floor. Her breaths exhaled loudly. *What the fuck just happened?* She'd never pegged Davie for the possessive type. It was a big red flag for her. She'd never dealt with a true Alpha male before, and she didn't want to, if he was going to get all Tarzan and Jane on her. But she didn't really think Davie was capable of being that way – did she? She was getting cold sitting on the floor. Her body was shaking. Maybe it was from going from super turned on to super annoyed faster than a jet hits speed.

She dropped her head back, letting it rest on the door. The worst of it was, she'd only gone on a date with Logan because she couldn't get Davie out of her mind; she didn't know if it was just being there that had her off track. But she couldn't tell him that, she couldn't tell him that ever since she'd arrived, her whole body seemed to crave his. That whenever he stood next to her, she had to hold her groin back from being pulled by gravitation, as though it was being called home.

The door banged, bouncing against her head.

Her breath caught; her stomach spun out of control. She turned as she stood up and pulled on the handle, slowly peered around it. Davie was there, a big hulk of a man, long hair, angry scowl, breath heaving, enveloped in the dark night. To anyone else this might have looked like something out of a horror movie. She, on the other hand, couldn't have been happier to see him.

"I'm not a jealous man," he growled. "I've never felt like I was losing my mind until I met you. I just can't bear the thought…"

He didn't finish his sentence before she had ploughed into him. He lifted her up and she wrapped her legs around his waist like she was climbing a tree. He wasted no time, kissing her deeply, feeling the warmth of her mouth and nibbling her bottom lip. He walked inside, Maisy still attached to him. He pressed her against the wall and kissed into her neck, his hands through her hair. She pushed back her head, enjoying the feel of his lips along her throat and up her chin. He groaned and her thighs tightened; she could feel the hardening bulge pressing against her. He leaned back and looked into her eyes, then he lifted her up further so that she was sitting on his chest and neck muscles. She was losing control, unravelling and they hadn't even undressed yet.

\*\*\*

Maisy woke up wrapped up in her sheets, Davie's heavy arm over her stomach. His head laid in her armpit, his soft breaths warm against her bare skin. His eyes opened and found hers.

"Good morning, beautiful."

She smiled. "Good morning." She stretched her arms and sighed. "It feels like the best night's sleep since I've been here, despite having little to no room."

"Well, you were pretty tired out."

She grinned. "I don't think I've ever experienced anything like that."

"Challenge accepted," he said, rolling over and blowing a raspberry into her chest. He leaned back his head and looked at her, grinning.

"What time is it?" she asked.

He reached over and picked up his phone. The next thing she knew she was flying through the air and toppling onto the ground. He scooped her up.

"Shit, I'm so sorry! Are you okay?"

She nodded and rubbed her knee where it had banged the edge of the bed. He placed her down and kissed her knee. She wiggled as the wiry hairs of his beard travelled up her core, he kissed her breasts, her throat and over her face, before swiftly standing himself back up. Then he grabbed his combat trousers and pulled them up over his legs.

"You're a bad influence. It's 7am, I've missed my morning run." He collected his T-shirt from the bedside cabinet, maintaining eye contact with her. He smirked shyly.

She laid watching him, the muscle that formed a line in the top of his shoulders, his pecs and then the ones that travelled from his stomach down into his pubic area. *My god, he is like a Fendi dress in a second-hand shop.*

"I'm also late for work. I have to be at the farm to help Alfie before giving Bob his medication."

She sat up with the sheet wrapped around her chest. "How about I give Bob his medication this morning? It is, after all, the main reason I'm here."

He leant down and kissed her tenderly on the forehead. Then he shook his head in disbelief. "Fucking gorgeous." He sighed as he walked out of the door.

"Wait! So, do you want me to go or not?" she called. He had already left. She flopped back onto the bed, missing the comfort of his warm, solid body next to hers.

\*\*\*

Bob was in his usual spot when she arrived, drinking a cup of coffee.

"You're early."

"Yes, I didn't know if Davie was coming this morning."

"Davie comes every morning. Although he was in a rush and said he'd have to give our game of chess a miss today."

"That's okay. Once we've done a bit of physio, you can show me how to play it," she said, opening the medicine cabinet. Her phone bleeped. She pulled it from her pocket and held it in her hand.

"You're on," said Bob. "I'm sick of getting beat by Davie everyday anyway. The man's a show-off."

She laughed at that. Then she opened her phone.

Miles: *Have you heard the news?*

She replied instantly. *No, what?*

She walked into the library with Bob's vitamins and water on his tiny wooden tray. "I've had my meds already," he said.

"I can see that; I just need to give you your multivitamin. You're actually running a little low," she said, shaking the pot.

"I know well, Davie took the repeat prescriptions with him this morning so maybe he's going to do a run."

"Doesn't miss a trick, does he?"

"No. Carey was the same. He might not be Carey's blood, but he still takes after her. He'll look after you too, I'm sure." He smirked.

"I'm sure he would." She grinned, passing him his vitamin and a glass of water. Her phone bleeped.

Miles: *Apparently, the mystery pooper returned again the other night and did some more damage. Looks like you're off the hook.*

She typed out a reply: *Did they find who did it?*

Miles: *No, but who cares? It proves it wasn't you!*

\*\*\*

She played chess whilst Bob told her more stories about Carey, they went for a walk around the garden discussing the progress so far, she then heard more stories about Carey. In the afternoon, Maisy and Angie changed all of the beds and cleaned the house. She made her way back to Corinuck feeling tired and satisfied. When she got back there was a note on her front door.

*Dinner at The Barn house, Main Street. (Behind the old farmhouse.) 6pm. D.*
*Come in your wellies!*

She looked at her watch. "It's 5.45pm now!" She chortled, running through the kitchen, throwing her clothes wherever they landed. She put her leg up on the sink, rubbed soap on it and ran a razor up her leg.

Normally, she would spend hours preening herself for a date. Instead, she had stripped off, washed herself at the sink and wore only mascara and lip gloss on her face. She slipped into a casual short Claudie Pierlot T-shirt dress with the unattractive wellington boots she was becoming accustomed to. It was a fair spring day, and she wasn't about to stuff herself up in a jumper. She glanced in the mirror. Her skin looked fresh and pink, and her hair had curled naturally. *It will have to stay this way.* She didn't look half bad in such a short space of time.

At 6.04pm she began her march back up the hill.

Davie had told her that his house was actually in the grounds of the old farm. When she got to the farmhouse, she went through the gate and past the garden entrance. She stood at the back, but she saw nothing. She went over a stile and looked out over the fields. There was a building of some sort at the other end of the field, but she couldn't tell if that was it. She spun on her heel, looking all around.

"Looking for something?" came a voice behind her. It was Logan. He was standing in Bob's garden; JD ran over and immediately started yapping at her.

"Oh hey, I'm just, err, looking for Davie. How have you been?" she stuttered, trying to work out what to say.

"Good. Great." He leaned back and folded his arms. He was wearing Boss sunglasses and a navy polo shirt. He was still wearing shorts, but he looked fresh with his hair slicked back and his eyebrows shaped and filled in. He was the complete opposite of Davie. Davie, who wore flannel shirts, combat trousers and big dirty boots.

"Good," she replied, rocking back on the heels of her boots.

"You look lovely."

"Thanks. I suppose I better go and find Davie," she said.

He paused. "Have you tried his house? Over there." He pointed at the building she'd spotted in the distance.

"Aha, thanks." She swung her leg over the stile, being sure to hold a hand down on her skirt.

Troy jogged over the garden, close to the fence. "Maisy?" he called. Maisy stopped and looked at him. "How come I haven't heard from you?" he asked.

"Sorry, I've been so busy," she said awkwardly.

He rubbed his fingers together, suddenly losing the confidence he always had. "Did I do something wrong?" he asked, pushing his sunglasses up onto his head.

"No." She really didn't want to go through it then, she was already late. "Let's catch up next time you're in town. Have a proper chat."

"Well, I'm here now. We could go to the Bull for a pint?"

"I'm actually late."

"Late for what? You said you were looking for Davie."

"Err."

His shoulder sagged. "So, it's true. You're seeing *him*?"

"I don't know what it is yet."

"Oh, come on, Maisy, he's not your type and you know it."

"And you are?"

"I believe I am, yes. We'd make beautiful babies together."

"Oh. You're wanting to settle down and make babies, are you?"

"One day," he said quietly.

She wanted to tell him that Davie was sweet, kind, thoughtful and that he made her laugh. Instead, she smiled and walked away.

"I'll be waiting when you get bored of him!" he called out behind her.

"Please don't," she shouted back, stepping over a cowpat.

The building she'd seen from a distance was a very quaint house. Huge white bricks with an oak wooden door and a large wooden decking that went almost all of the way around the house. In front of the open door stood Davie and his dog by his bare feet.

He slipped a phone from his back pocket and took a picture of her approaching before she'd even realised what he was doing. His long hair was tied back, his beard was oiled. He was wearing baggy jeans and a clean white muscle vest, showing off his bulging traps. She felt her blood pressure rise.

"Fuck me!" she whispered to herself as she traipsed closer, dodging shit. "Where have you been hiding all my fucking life?"

She got closer. "Did you say something?" he asked.

"No. Did you just take a picture of me?"

"I did, the contrast suits you. I needed something for the bank." He wiggled his eyebrows and she laughed, feeling a hot spark in the pit of her stomach.

"I assume yours isn't a calm bank?"

He raised an eyebrow. "No, actually, quite the opposite."

"Did you oil your beard?"

"I did! First time ever! Hugh gave me it! His niece brought him it for Christmas and he said that she told him everyone does it in London. Is that true?"

"Lots of people do use the stuff; looks great on you. But don't change yourself for me, Davie."

"I know who I am, don't you worry about that."

She stepped onto the decking. He looked her up and down like he was hungry and she was his prey. He kissed her on the cheek; a small growl escaped his lips as he did. She felt her knees weaken.

"Tell me you eat meat?" he asked, following her inside.

"I do," she replied, her voice gravelly.

"Beef?"

"Yes."

"I've made minced beef and tatties."

"What are tatties?"

"You know tatties. They grow out of the ground."

"Potatoes?"

"Aye. Tatties."

"Sounds good to me."

"It's one of Bob's favourites, with a touch of my own twist."

She walked inside and pulled off her boots.

"Can't you keep them on? I was thinking how sexy you looked in them."

She laughed. "No, they're filthy. And this wooden flooring is immaculate," she marvelled.

He led her inside. The floors, walls and furniture were a contrast of dark-and-white clean wooden panelling. With pictures of the highland cows, sheep and lakes dotted around. The fireplace was open and black and white with a wall stocked full of logs.

"Davie! You've been holding out on me. This house is gorgeous."

He glanced back at her. "What did you expect?" He let out a *tch*. "Maisy? You expected me to live in a cow shed, didn't you?"

She hesitated. "Not exactly," she murmured. "I thought more like a small scruffy little bachelor pad. Should have known, I suppose."

She followed him into a stylish kitchen with a huge island where he'd got vegetables prepared ready for the crock pot. He slid a glass of red wine over the table.

"Do you like red?"

"I do, it gets me a little tipsy though."

"I heard it goes well with red meat. And I'll try not to judge if you find yourself having a little singsong later then."

"I appreciate that, and I am impressed – I didn't realise you were so sophisticated."

"Aye don't get used to it. I normally have haggis and OJ."

"Not whiskey?"

"Cannae stand the stuff." She screwed up her face. "I know. I know. I'm a traitor to my own culture," Davie replied, grinning. He raised his own glass. "To new friends."

She clinked her glass against his and took a sip.

She watched him cooking barefoot in his oddly up-to-date kitchen and sipped her wine. She typed out a text to Ameera. *Did you hear the latest? Michael's car was smashed up again.* She pressed send. She looked up. "Can I do anything to help?" she asked.

"It's all in hand, darling. You just sit there and look fooking stunning as you are."

"God, I could just listen to you talk all day." She sighed.

"Well, that's good cus most English people find my accent fucking annoying."

"I doubt that very much."

"You'd be surprised. But then again, I find a lot of people annoying myself."

She laughed and took another gulp of wine.

She glanced at her phone; the message hadn't sent. She placed it down on the counter, telling herself to forget about it for now. Davie reached behind him; he slid a Wi-Fi card over to her.

"There. Now that'll be two places around here where you get Wi-Fi," he said with a grin.

They ate dinner at a small table by floor-to-ceiling glass doors that looked out over the rolling fields. Maisy was shovelling food into her mouth when she looked up and caught Davie watching her. Grinning.

"Enjoying it?" he asked, one eyebrow raised.

"Sorry." She laughed through a mouthful of food.

"Are you kidding? I love to see a woman enjoying her food. Especially when I cooked it."

She gave him a wide smile. Feeling sauce on her lips she stuck out her tongue and licked it up. Davie winked at her.

She grinned back at him and shook her head. "You're full of surprises! The food is delectable."

"Delectable, eh?" He beamed.

She glanced out of the window. A few hundred yards behind his house she saw stalls, a horse's head poking out.

"Oh wow. You have horses?" she screeched.

"Well, they're Bob's but yes. You ride?"

"I had lessons as a kid." He raised an eyebrow in response. "Yep, I also did girls' football, karate, boxing, tennis, baking, chess club, dance. Then there was: ballet, acting, gymnastics, life-saving swimming and... archery. But horse riding was my favourite and longest-lasting hobby. Everything else was fairly short-lived."

He gasped and shook his head.

"You did all that?"

"Yep."

"Wow. Well, we can ride on Sunday if ya fancy it?"

"Absolutely, I would love that!" she exclaimed. "As a kid, I always wanted to be a vet. I've always got on better with animals than people."

He shook his head. "Yeah, I could see you as a vet. In your little white coat with animals all around you." She laughed. "But in all seriousness, I get what ya saying, Maisy. Animals somehow calmed me too. It's like they see right through you.

"Exactly! Not everyone understands that."

"They don't." He smiled easily. "I still can't believe how much you did as a kid. Your parents really wanted to give you life skills, eh?"

She sipped her wine and looked at him over the rim of her glass. "I think they just wanted me to behave. To put it politely, I was an energetic child. I was hard work, still am sometimes. I barely slept and didn't make, or keep, friends too easily. I was a bit too much for them to handle. And they had money too and a reputation to upkeep. My mum was a magazine editor, my dad was in the building trade. So, I suppose they found ways to keep me busy and out of trouble – that way I couldn't embarrass them." She chewed another mouthful, then stopped mid-chew and looked up at him. "Oh god, did I barf my life on you? I was rambling, I'm sorry."

"Not at all. Don't apologise to me, you're an interesting person, city girl."

"I normally don't share so much of myself."

"Well then, I feel honoured."

She laughed. "You shouldn't be."

"I think that's a matter of opinion. You're like a breath of fresh air."

"Are you drunk?" she said with a laugh.

His eyes locked with hers, his glass played at his lips. "I'm serious. You bring life to the everyday mundane. You light up every room you walk into."

Maisy felt choked by his words. She tried to swallow down the lump that had developed in her throat. She ran her fork through the remaining green beans and potatoes on her plate.

"And you... have an ability to see the good in everything." Her bottom lip quivered.

"I only see what I see. And I think you're exceptional. If I'm honest, I'd never in a million years expect a woman like you to go for me. I know who I am. I'm old-fashioned and stuck in my ways."

"But you've hit the nail on the head there. You know who you are. You're solid and strong. The opposite to me – flaky and emotional."

"I think your sensitivity is endearing, not a weakness."

She shivered. He *saw* her, she realised. And he didn't realise what men their age were like. She'd met more of them than she cared to remember. None of them were like him, none of them felt like home the way he did.

"You getting cold, lass?"

"Oh erm, just a little," she said, wondering if it was more a reaction to his words more than the temperature. He was lucky she hadn't started crying again. She followed him into the lounge and he lit the fire. There was a guitar hanging on the wall.

"You play?"

"I can play two songs." He smirked, holding up two fingers. "The classic's 'Auld Lang Syne' and 'Smells Like Teen Spirit'. You know either of them?"

"I do. I know them both."

"Guitar lessons weren't in your list of skills?"

"No, but I did play the piano for a while."

He chuckled like he knew her in a way that made him feel familiar and mysterious all at the same time. The sound was like dipping into a hot bath after a hard day. She plonked herself down onto his sofa, holding her wine glass up. Tennant jumped up and curled around on the spot, dropping onto her knee. She placed her spare hand on the dog's head and nuzzled behind his ear. Her phone pinged.

Ameera: *Yep, I did hear about Michael's car. Crazy, hey. So, how's Outlander life going?*

She replied: *I hope they catch whoever did it. All good here. Will call soon, miss you.*

She looked up. Davie placed his wine glass on top of the fireplace and grabbed his guitar.

"I'll play for you. But you can't laugh, okay?"
"Why would I laugh?!"
"Because I'm a bit rusty. It's been a while."

He began to play the chords of the Nirvana song she recognised so well, and she melted. It all felt so surreal, the house, the man, the fire and the view of the countryside; her body was floating. He placed the guitar on the floor and took a sip of wine. She stood up, placed hers on the shelf and walked over to him nervously. She stood in front of him, and he looked up at her. She sat on his lap, wrapping her legs around his him and she kissed his lips. He kissed her back eagerly. Her tongue played around the edge of his lips, he nibbled at hers in return. She leant back to look into his eyes.

"I'd have played sooner if I knew I was that good!"

They chuckled together; his forehead pressed against hers. He pulled her chest to his and kissed her again. Her head rocked back, exposing her throat. He licked and kissed it gently, sending goose bumps up her spine. She leant down to him; this kiss was much more tender, slower, and intense than the last. Without thinking anymore into it, she reached up and pulled her dress over her head, then pulled off his vest. She felt herself melt into his body. He stood up and carried her up the stairs to his bedroom.

# Fifteen

They marched into the garden from the fields. The sun was going down behind them.

She turned and looked at him grinning, her whole face lit up. "That was so much fun. I'd forgotten how much I love getting out in the country like that. The wind in my hair, the smell of the tree's"

"You were great. I was expecting you to need some help after all this time. But you were like a natural."

"Oh. I felt it at first, but as I relaxed my body just took over. It helps that Clyde was so well trained. He's a delight to ride."

He crept up behind her and wrapped an arm around her waist, lifting her as he buried his mouth into her neck. "I'm a fucking delight to ride," he responded into her ear. He swung her around, as she giggled. He raised his eyebrows at her, nibbling his bottom lip. She smiled. They clambered inside; the radio he'd left on for Tennant was playing an old NSYNC song. Maisy wiggled to the tune as she pulled off her boots.

"That's it!" he growled. He ran over, picked her up and

threw her over his shoulder. "Oh, you're getting it now," he said. She giggled. He had one hand on her arse, one hanging limp by his side. He pulled off his own boots, then hurried up the stairs. She screamed with delight.

"You're an animal," she called jerkily.

"I'll show you a fucking animal." He threw her down onto the bed and began dancing over her as he stripped off his clothes. She threw back her head. He'd never heard a woman laugh so much.

# Sixteen

The chicken breast was cooked to perfection. Davie took it out to the dining room and placed it on the table between the potatoes and vegetables.

"The pair of you have done us proud. This all looks beautiful," said Hilda.

"Agreed," said Bob.

"The lass is obviously a good influence," added Hugh.

"I'm a good influence on her, more like." He laughed and nudged her with his arse as they took a seat.

She grinned and he remembered her laying in his bed grinning that way the night before. She laughed at something, and he looked up; she was chatting with Hilda, and he felt a contentment rising inside of him. He was falling for her, he realised. What the fuck was he going to do now?

"I see you went out on the horses yesterday?" Bob asked.

"We did. She's a natural, she did so well." He side-eyed her. "It was great to see," he said, then he noticed her blush a little. He wondered if she was remembering afterwards, like he was.

At the table with all the elders, the last thing he needed was big man waking up. He tried to think of something else, but the thoughts of her were spinning through his mind, as though on replay. Fuck! He was like a horny teenager all over again. It was torture.

He looked down at his food and started chewing. *Chew, chew, chew*, he thought in a singsong voice. That was when Hilda threw a bucket of cold water on his thoughts.

"What are your plans now, Maisy? With Bob being so much better now?"

Davie's head bolted up and Maisy turned and met his gaze, her eyes wide and frightened. Then she turned back to Hilda. "Well, I only have three weeks left anyway."

*Three fooking weeks left! Where has the time gone?*

"But if my work is done here, and Angie has no more work for me… then I suppose I will head home soon."

And just like that, he felt his insides crumbling in on itself. He'd reminded himself over and over that she was temporary. When had he forgotten that?

"What made you volunteer here anyway? Do you have another job?" asked Hilda.

"No, I chose to volunteer here, so that I could gain some clarity over what I want to do for a living. I also wanted to help, of course."

"At your age?" Hilda asked. "How on earth do you support yourself, financially?"

"Hilda!" chastised Bob. He turned to Maisy. "If it helps, Maisy, I think a caring career suits you perfectly."

"Thanks, Bob. I honestly didn't know I'd enjoy it so much. I'm contemplating going back to college, maybe training to be a vet. I know I'm a little old…"

"You're never too old to go back to school," said Hugh.

She grinned at him and turned to Hilda. "In answer to your question Hilda – I'm lucky enough to have parents who have supported me. Now I need to get out into the real world and start a career of my own."

"Well, you should do it now, before you're too old. That biological clock must be ticking by now," Hilda said.

Maisy scoffed.

"What do ya parents do, lass?" asked Bob.

"My dad owns a building company called Fowler's Homes, have you heard of it?"

"Naw."

"Oh well, it's based in Leicester, but they have gangs of builders putting up houses all over the country. And then my mum, she was an editor for a magazine called *City Life* but she's a housewife now. The house got so big it became a full-time job keeping it." She sniggered.

"And your dad hasn't hired you to work for him?"

"No." She twiddled her hair in her fingers. "It can be complicated working with your family, can't it?"

"Aye," agreed Bob. "Although, this one here was nothing but a credit to the farm," he said, indicating at Davie with his head.

"You've obviously raised him with good morals, Bob. He's a very conscientious man."

Davie could hear the smile in her voice, see that she had turned his way, but he didn't look back at her, he couldn't. He stared ahead, quietly eating his food, hoping to go unnoticed as he listened to the conversation, a sick feeling in the pit of his stomach.

Afterwards, they all gathered around for a game of rummy, but Davie wasn't in the mood to join in. He wanted to be alone. He offered to wash the pots and pottered around, keeping busy as they played. He did not want time to think about the searing pain inside of his chest.

He hadn't thought about the inevitable until now because he didn't want to face it, but by spending more time with her he was heading into heartbreak territory. It was time for him to get his head out of the sand. Bob walked in.

Davie forced a smile. "Look at you, walking around. It's like you're ten years younger, Bob."

"I know. Doc's putting my tablets down. I'm like a new man."

"What's done that? Is it all from the physio?"

He paused for a moment and leaned on the counter. "No, Davie. It's you and her."

"What? That is ridiculous. So suddenly because I'm getting laid, you've made a miraculous recovery?" He smirked.

"No, not that you idiot. She got me talking about Carey. You did the garden where I can go to speak to her. I've been reading up on it. Your body can experience real physical pain from heartbreak. "

Didn't he know it; his was breaking already and Maisy was still there.

"And besides, Maisy isn't just getting laid. I know when my own son is in love."

He'd only called him son a few times, usually in proud moments and every time it had gripped his heart. But the old man was crazy if he thought Davie was in love! He'd known from the start that Maisy was temporary. *We're having fun!* he told himself. But the voice in the back of his mind asked, *then why are you in here sulking, whilst she is out there playing cards?*

"How's it going between you two, anyway?" Bob asked.

"Fine," he said, his façade beginning to crumble.

Bob grabbed Davie's arm, his hand shaking. "You can't fool me. If it's fine, then why are ya hiding in here?"

Davie grinned at the same question he was asking himself. "I'm just washing up," he murmured.

Bob gave him a stern look. "We have a dishwasher, laddie."

Davie pressed his lips into a thin line. "She's just said it herself; she's leaving soon Bob." Davie propped the pan he had scrubbed to oblivion onto the draining board.

"Do you want me to be ill again, cus I reckon I could fake it, if I need to."

Davie grinned then. "I don't want her here against her will, Bob."

"Aye, I suppose not. So, there's only one other thing to do."

"What's that?"

"Fetch me the box down from off that cupboard," he said, pointing at the hallway unit. Davie hesitated, then dried his hands on the tea towel and went to get the box. He placed it down on the dining table, hearing the whoops coming from the study as they played the game. Bob shuffled his shaky hands inside the box, then pulled out a smaller navy-blue box and opened it. Davie's throat dried.

"That's Carey's wedding ring," he croaked.

"Exactly. And she'd have wanted nothing more than you to be happy."

"I am not proposing to a woman I have been with for twenty bloody weeks."

"You'd be an idiot not to. You love her and she loves you."

There was a shuffle of feet. Davie grabbed the ring box, shut it, and shoved it into his pocket.

"Everything okay?" asked Maisy. He gulped guiltily, praying she hadn't heard anything of their ridiculous conversation.

"Aye, we're just having a chat. We'll be in in a minute, lass. Does everyone want a cuppa tea?"

She hesitated and nervously looked around at Bob. She wanted to say something, he could tell. She opened her mouth. "More than likely but I'll go and ask round."

"Great," he responded, watching her walk back out. "I mean it, Davie, don't let her slip through your fingers," Bob grumbled, shuffling away.

Davie turned around to fill the kettle with water.

"You should at least ask her to stay," Bob continued, as he disappeared around the door, leaving only the noise of his shuffling shoes. Davie leant onto the kitchen counter and sighed. He couldn't propose… could he? No, it was flipping ridiculous! And besides, she was the one leaving. He'd be better off just keeping away, protecting his heart. He didn't think he could face being around her anymore, knowing that she was going to leave him.

# Seventeen

Maisy turned off the clunky tap, washing the last few pots, her yellow rubber gloves squeaking together as she rubbed. Bob had walked several laps of the garden and had gone for a lay down; she couldn't believe how well he was doing. She placed his medicine syringe on the draining board, looking out at Davie's house in the distance. She missed him so much it hurt her insides. She didn't know what was bothering Davie. But she was certain it was something to do with the conversation he'd had in the kitchen with Bob. Because afterwards, he'd walked her home in complete silence and he'd told her he had to go, before kissing her on the forehead. The forehead for god's sake. That was how you kissed a nephew or a grandma, not someone who had enjoyed every part of you.

He obviously had some things to work out. So, she'd done the honourable thing, she had stepped back and given him some space, despite being aware that they were on a time constraint. She thought he'd be back after one or two days, but she'd heard nothing. Then again, she'd thought it was only a bit of fun. She'd be going home soon and she'd never see him again. But days of walking the garden and listening to Bob's stories of the past. Days of Corinuck's creaks and cracks and night-time howls that she was becoming so familiar with. Days of Illvenie without him in it, had made her realise it was more than fooling around to her. She wanted more. How could she be so foolish? She'd never been in this situation before, would this pass? She thought about calling Roxy, asking her. She needed to do something; she just didn't know what.

"Maisy?" called Bob.

"Yeah?" She walked out of the kitchen, through the hallway, following the sound of his voice into the study.

"You, okay?" Maisy asked. Bob was sat in his comfy chair across to Hugh. They were opening the chessboard.

"You can go now, lovey. Don't need to be hanging around here."

She scanned through the books. "You're feeling okay?"

"Yep," Bob replied, only now he sounded genuine.

"It was a pretty big walk for you today," she responded.

"Stop worrying, lass. I'm good. And Angie will be popping in with dinner in an hour or two."

"Okay," she said absently.

She picked up a veterinary book and started reading the blurb. Bob and Hugh finished setting up the board. She skimmed the pages of the book. Bob moved his pawn.

"Unless you're hanging around for a reason, Maisy?" Bob said, grinning.

She turned and looked at him. "No, Bob, I'm not waiting for Davie if that's what you think." She closed the book onto her open hand. Bob raised his eyebrows at her. "I never said a word about Davie, lass."

Hugh grinned, popping a mint into his mouth.

"Actually, would it be okay if I sat on the veranda upstairs and read this book?" Maisy asked. "I'm just waiting for a call from my mum and have no reception anywhere else."

"Of course, Maisy, you know you're welcome here anytime."

\*\*\*

The veranda had a small mosaic table and two chairs; the view from there was gorgeous. She could almost see the whole village, plus the fields went down and expanded for miles. She inhaled and exhaled deeply, her hand on her ribs; she felt a calm wash over her.

She imagined Davie sweeping back his hair, the way he wiggled his nose, the words he'd said. *You're in the calmest place on earth right now. This view alone is therapy, you don't need Butt-yakee or whatever it is. In fact, lets name it Illvee-yakee therapy.*

*Illvee-yakee therapy.*

She thought about her family and Ameera and Roxy. It would be time to go home soon. She imagined walking in and hugging everyone. She'd missed them all, she missed Ameera. Ameera had always been the one Maisy turned to in times of need, and she'd always come up with solutions that empowered her. She slipped her phone from the back pocket of her jeans and dialled.

"What the fuck is wrong with you? I swear down, man, if this guy's not turning up with diamonds begging for you, yeah? Forget about him and come home. Come home anyways. We'll go out and find you a real man. Even if we don't find you a man right away, we'll have a bloody good time finding you one, innit?"

Maisy rolled her eyes. She'd heard the saying 'distance makes the heart grow fonder' but did it also make the heart grow distant or alien?

"I don't want another man. I like this one." Maisy groaned.

"So, what you gonna do. Stop there now?" Ameera asked.

"No, but being away has made me think. There's nothing left for me back home. And I am starting to like it here."

"Maisy, what are you talking about, man? You told me a couple of weeks ago; there are no salons, no shopping centres, no nightclubs, no job opportunities, not even fucking 3G in most places. Have you lost your mind? Do I need to come there myself and drag you home? Cus if I have to, I will. I might be accused of being some things, yeah, but a bad friend ain't one of them. If you need me to come and drag you back, then I will."

"I don't need dragging back. I really like it here. I really like Davie."

"You don't even know him, man. Don't get trapped in a dead-end place like that. With a bunch of Neanderthals. Come back where there's loads of opportunities."

Maisy remembered a time when she used to look up to Ameera. She was so straight shooting and ballsy. Now, listening to her, she sounded different. Like someone she didn't know, and she couldn't put a finger on it. Could you outgrow someone in a matter of weeks?

"The people here are not Neanderthals, they're smart and they're my friends."

"Maisy, man, I didn't want to be the one to say it, but these people are changing you. It's as though you're living in a cult, and they're brainwashing you into staying and being some kind of weird housewife in their community. You need to come home and get your head straight."

"What?" She gasped. "They don't even know I want to stay. They may not even have room for me."

"That's what they want you to think, man. Honestly, I've watched documentaries about this kind of thing, in the mountains in America and places like that. No one says the mountain people of Scotland are any better."

"Ameera, you really don't know what you're talking about. Please just stop."

"Miles told me you'd gone all weird and naturalistic and I didn't believe him. I was like nah not our Maisy, she'd never let herself go. But now I'm starting to wonder. Just tell me something, yeah?"

"What?"

"What are you wearing right now?"

"Why does it matter what I'm wearing?"

"See! The real Maisy would never say that. You've been brainwashed, man. It's not your fault, you just don't realise it. And you need me to come and exorcise them demons or some shit."

Maisy started laughing. "Ameera!" she yelled. "Get a grip! You're talking like a crazy person. Have you been smoking too much weed again? Wait, someone's trying to call. Sorry, Meer, I have to go."

She picked up the call.

"Maisy Fowler?"

"Yes."

"Hi, this is PC Jones from Leicestershire constabulary. I just wanted to let you know that all charges have been dropped against you in reference to Juniper Road. As we have now found the culprit in question."

"You have? Who did it?"

"Well, I suppose in this case I can actually tell you the identity of the guilty party. Her name is Gerty."

"Gerty?"

"Yes, she's an old English Goat."

"What?"

"Yes, it turns out she keeps going missing from her home, a mile away. Mr Montell had hanging baskets above his car that she seemed to like the taste of. She was caught on camera returning to the scene of the crime this week."

"It was a goat! After all that. A damn goat." She laughed.

Maisy called home, to let them know the good news.

"That's brilliant news. So, are you coming home now?" asked Miles.

She scowled. "No! My job here isn't quite finished!"

"To be fair, Maisy, I'm shocked you've made it this far," he said with a laugh.

In a single moment the feelings of being home, surrounded by people who had no hope for her, all came flooding back. What was she going to do? Look for another volunteer job somewhere else?

She felt anger rising through her body, heating up her face. She looked out over the rolling fields. She inhaled deeply.

*Illvee-yakee*, she thought with a grin.

"You know what, Miles?" she snapped, then took a

deep breath in... *Illvee-yakee.* Her voice calmed. "I didn't think I'd make it here either. The first couple of nights were sketchy. The house was like a shed in the middle of the field on its own. Did you know that deer growl?"

"What?"

"Honestly, they growl. Sounds like a mixture of a frog and a ferocious animal."

"You're kidding!" He laughed. A tear ran down her face as they chatted like two adults.

"Hey, I'm sorry. I know I've been selfish. When I come home, I'm going to work on being a better person."

"I'm sorry too, Maisy. And for the record, I think you've already started that journey. I'm proud of you."

"Send my love to Mum and Dad. How are they, by the way?"

"They're good. Dad's taken up tennis, believe it or not, and he's actually losing weight. I'd never tell him that, of course, but, between me and you, I think it's doing him good."

She smiled to herself and stood up, looking down the road. A soft breeze rushed over her face and through her hair. She wondered if she would see Davie arriving home.

"It was nice speaking to you, Maisy." He said, actually sounding genuine.

"You too, Miles."

She picked the book up off the table, opened the page to 'pet pathology', sat back, and tried to focus on the words on the page. She felt as though a sheet of calm had gently dropped down over her.

When the day began to close in, Maisy wandered inside, locked the door, and made her way downstairs. She walked into the study to place the book back on the shelf.

Hilda was listening to jazz quietly and circling around the room, ball dancing with an invisible partner. Hugh was seated in the corner.

"Evening, Hilda. Evening, Hugh."

"Hey there, Maisy."

"Where's Bob this evening?"

"He's in the garden with Angie."

She glanced at her watch. "But it's 8pm."

"Yes, well, Davie's only just left.

"He was here?"

"Yes. Poor lad looked exhausted."

Maisy felt herself blush. She made her way through the house in a blur, she stepped outside into the garden. Her breath hitched in her throat. He wasn't there, but what was, took her breath away.

"It's finished!" she squealed. "When did he finish the flower beds?" She turned to Bob who was sat on the bench with Angie, and if she wasn't mistaken, he looked as though he'd been crying. She dropped onto the bench beside him, looking at the flowers blooming all around them of all colours, shapes, and sizes.

"This is how she loved it," Bob said, turning to look at her, his face blotchy. She hugged him until he took a deep breath.

"When did he finish this?" she asked again.

"He was here all day and all night on Wednesday, then he finished it today. I think it was more for you than for me if I'm honest, but its magical."

Angie stood up. "I'll get you a hot chocolate before bed, Bob. Want one, Maisy?"

"No, I'm okay thank you, Ang."

Maisy released a lung full of air.

Bob nodded at Angie, then turned to Maisy, a look of sincerity on his face. "Thanks, love," he said.

"Me?" Maisy laughed. "What did I do?"

"You asked him to do it, you opened his eyes, you brought my boy back to life." He paused to inhale through his mouth. "When a man is in love, he will go to lengths, eh?"

"It's beautiful. He did a great job." She said, sighing. "But Davie is not in love with me, Bob. He did it in honour of Carey. And for you, of course."

He chuckled at that and shook his head.

"I don't think he even likes me right now," she said, raising her eyebrows.

"Oh, Maisy, and I thought I was the daft old sod. He's not talking to you because you're leaving him and it's breaking his heart."

Her stomach sunk. *That can't be true, can it?*

"What makes you think that, Bob?"

"Because he told me so. Right there in the kitchen the night we all had that delicious meal together."

*The night Davie started being distant with me.*

She sat up and leaned forward. "He actually said that he loved me?"

"Well, no… but he might as well have done. What was it he said?" He sat rubbing his chin.

Maisy leaned back, her hope fading. Angie came walking back outside and handed a steaming mug to Bob, carefully placing it into his open hands.

Maisy looked up at her. "I'm going to go soon. Do you need some help getting Bob inside?" She asked.

Angie looked at Bob and then at Maisy.

"Maisy, he walked out here unaided. I was leaving when I thought I'd better keep an eye on him, but he didn't need me."

"Oh my god, that's amazing! Bob, it's a breakthrough."

"Like a new man!" He grinned.

She hugged him, careful not to squeeze his delicate bones too tight. "I've got to get some sleep but I'm so happy for you, Bob! You're doing better every day."

"All the better for having your help, my dear," he said.

"I cannot take credit for that, you've done this."

"Not without you." He grinned. She headed for the door. "I remember now," he said. She looked back and leaned on the open frame, looking at him expectantly. "What he actually said was that he couldn't keep you here if you didn't want to stay. But the idea of you leaving felt like being plunged into darkness."

Her breath caught in the back of her throat. She looked at Angie.

"Don't look at me, lassie. I wasn't here."

She moved closer to Bob.

"Are you sure that's what he said?"

"Aye."

"They were his exact words?"

"His exact words."

"What do I do?" She said, panting, almost breathless.

"If you feel the same, I suggest you get round there and tell him! He thinks you don't want him."

"I don't know what I should say or feel; I don't think there's anything I can tell him." She said.

"Bloody kids." He said, sighing.

# Eighteen

"We used to have a maple tree here. Carey took a snippet of one from her grandma's garden and regrew it herself. She used to say that when she wanted to go back to her roots, she'd come out here and sit with the tree."

"What happened to it?"

"It died, I suppose."

"Hang on, Bob! That's perfect; we could plant a maple out here in memory of Carey. What kind of maple was it?"

"I'm not sure."

She typed 'red maple' into her phone's search engine. "Was it this one?"

She showed him the picture and he got closer to the screen, squinting. "No. The leaves were brighter. They were almost pink." She showed him another. "Aye, like that."

"Okay then. Now we just need to see if we can get one locally."

"There's a garden centre on the way to Inverness. Why don't you see if Davie will lend you his flat bed?"

"I don't know." Her stomach sank at the sound of his name. "I still haven't heard from Davie."

"Why haven't you been round to see him for goodness' sake? Do not tell me you don't feel the same way. I saw it on your face."

"We're from different worlds, Bob."

"Then stay in this one!"

"I won't have a job in two weeks. And besides, I don't have anywhere to live."

"Move in with Davie. With all this internet stuff these days I'm sure you could find something."

She looked at him sceptically.

"Move into the farm then, be our full-time carer. Hilda's getting a bit forgetful lately. I'd pay you a wee wage."

"Oh, Bob," she said, placing a hand on his arm.

"I have faith in the two of you." He said.

"We've only been seeing each other a few weeks. I know you want Davie to be happy but how can you really be sure? We live completely different lives, we're completely different people and even if we could see past that… I'd mess everything up eventually, anyway. And then what? One of us has uprooted our lives for nothing. I know Carey was the love of your life but it will just never work for Davie and I."

"Oh, gobbledeygosh!"

Maisy realised they had reached the back door.

"Oh my god, Bob!" she exclaimed.

"What?"

"You've walked the whole garden and you don't even seem in pain."

"So I have." He looked around in wonder, his mouth half open. Then he looked at the floor. "My knees are hurting a bit. Perhaps I'd better sit down." Quickly, he began shuffling away. She grinned to herself then, following him to the garden bench.

***

"What is with the sour face? Just tell the girl how you feel!" Alfie demanded.

"There's nothing wrong with ma face. I'm just a little tired."

"Ach with ya."

Craig slammed two pints down in front of them; Alfie swiped his away. "He's got a point, Davie; you've been in here all week looking miserable as hell. How can telling her make it any worse than this?"

"Exactly," Alfie said, raising his pint, having already taken a gulp.

Davie put his hands into his jacket pocket, he'd been feeling around for the small box, he gripped it tight. "What is the point? I cannae leave Illvenie; there's too much to think about with work and Bob and my house. And you can't expect a towny to move here either, can you? It is a big adjustment. It'll never go anywhere."

"Surely you should give her that choice, Davie," Craig said.

The door behind them swung open, bringing with it a gush of wind.

Alfie started explaining Davie's non-existent love life to Craig in detail.

"Excuse me," came a female voice. "Can you please tell me where Coorie Nook is?"

The words had Davie swivelling on his bar stool faster

than a rabbit ran down a bolt hole. A woman ladled with bags was pushing her hair from her face, flustered. It reminded him of the day Maisy clambered into his life. The woman had coffee-coloured skin and long dark hair. Her high cheek bones were intensified by her pouting face. She was dressed in a black tight dress, the words 'Fendi' emblazoned down the sides, with white trainer boots with red hearts. Angie's brother Sam, who, two minutes ago had looked as though he was sleeping in the chair by the door, was staring up at her with his mouth open – visably dribbling. He didn't seem as though he was going to reply any time soon.

"Did you say Corinuck?" called Davie.

Her thin slits of emerald eyes sought him out. "Yeah, Coorie Nook."

Davie laughed aloud. Her eyes widened. "You a friend of Maisy's by any chance?" he asked.

She walked towards him. "You know her?"

"Davie," he said, putting out a hand for her to shake. A look of realisation dawned on her face.

"Ameera." Her voice softened and she seemed to be appraising him slowly, suddenly a loud voice he wasn't expecting came from her mouth. "Fucking hell. So, you're the bloke that's got her in turmoil, are you?"

Davie stared at her.

"What makes you say that?" Alfie asked, a frown on his face.

She dropped her bags, blocking the floor and lifted her bum up onto the stool. "Cus she ain't the Maisy I know and love. That's why I thought I'd better come down here and make sure nothing weirds going on, innit."

Craig was standing behind the bar, watching like they were the latest Netflix show. He leaned over and stuck out his hand. "I'm Craig. Welcome to Illvenie."

"Alright," she said, tapping his hand in an awkward sideways high-five.

"Maisy's with Angie," Davie spoke into his pint. "She'll be aboot an hour; you're welcome to join us for a pint though, Ameera."

"Don't mind if I do," she said, pushing her elbows into the bar and glancing around at them all enthusiastically.

"What'll you be having?"

"You buying, Davie? Lovely! I'll have a double rum and coke please."

He raised his eyebrows then turned around and nodded at Craig. Craig placed the drink down in front of her and leant over the bar until he was facing her. "So, funnily enough," he said, leaning in conspiratorially, "we we're just discussing your friend Maisy, before you blew in. You see, it's become clear to us all that Davie here is a little besotted with young Maisy, and we think she feels the same about him. And yet, neither of them will admit it. Don't you think our friend here should tell her how he feels?"

She took a sip of her drink, thoughtfully. "Nah, man. I'm sure he's a nice enough bloke 'n' all but Maisy is a bit flaky and spontaneous. If he does that, she'll probably do something stupid like move across the country to be with him. A few weeks in, she'll realise she don't even want him. Then she'll feel like shit, go through some weird depression and she will disappear into the night, and your friend here will be broken-hearted. Trust me, no one wants that."

Craig stood back up, crossing his arms and shaking his head. Davie thumped his fist down onto the bar. "My point exactly!" he said pointing at Craig. "Well sort of."

"Naw, hold on a minute," shouted Alfie. "This girl hasn't even seen you two together! How could she possibly know!"

"Yeah, she doesnee know."

Ameera started jumping in her seat. "You asked me!"

"I know but I was clearly misguided. Those beautiful eyes told me that you looked like someone who believed in love."

"Oh my god. I've never met such a bunch of naïve men before. C'mon, man! I believe in love, but I'm also a realist and I know Maisy. Me and her ain't made for settling down. We're just not the settling types."

Craig shivered in an exaggerated manner. "You know, I thought the temperature dropped when you walked in. You're like the devil, woman."

Ameera started laughing. "Has anyone ever told you that you've got this angry, sexy vibe going on?"

He winked at her as he went to fill another customer's glass. Davie grumbled and took another slug of his pint.

"Is this the only pub in town?" Ameera asked.

"It is," he replied.

"God, she must be drowning in a place like this."

Davie sat up. He looked at her, then at Craig. "She's right. A woman like Maisy needs more than I can offer here."

"You're wrong, Ameera," said Craig, taking Davie's empty glass over to the beer tap.

"Yup. I've seen how happy the two of you are when you're together," grumbled Alfie.

Ameera threw back her drink. "Well, it's been a pleasure, gents."

"Leaving already?" Craig asked. He pouted his bottom lip and flicked his eyelashes at her dramatically. She grinned back at him. She hopped off the stool. "I'm going to go and surprise my friend. But I'll be back."

"She'll be at Looch Farm," Davie said without turning to look at her.

"Thank you," she replied sweetly.

# Nineteen

Maisy walked out of Looch Farm with a sense of accomplishment. When she'd got there it had been dark, and when she was left it was dark too. But she didn't care, Bob had come so far; his medication had halved, and he was getting himself around again. She had been part of that. She had never felt like such a success.

She caught a glimpse of a shadow beyond the gate, and she slowed her pace as she squinted. There was a person sitting on the wall. But wait! It couldn't be, could it?

"Ameera!" she called, excited.

"Fucking hell man. Took you long enough, I'm freezing my tits off out here."

They ran to each other and jumped into a hug.

"Oh my god! What are you doing here?"

"You said your work was finished. I've come to make sure you leave this place."

"I have my car, and I can't officially finish until at least tomorrow evening."

As they stood in front of the light of the farm's kitchen window, Ameera took a step back.

"Oh my god, you look so different. Where are your hair extensions? Where are your lashes? What are those boots?" She asked, in disgust.

"Wellingtons!" Maisy replied defensively.

Ameera picked up Maisy's hand then dropped it raising her upper lip.

"And what the hell happened to your nails, man?"

"I don't need them here," she said, grinning.

"But you've let yourself go!"

Maisy's face screwed up. "I feel good," she said, touching her face self-consciously. "I'm still mad at you, by the way."

"Yeah, I know. You can never be mad at me for long though."

They strolled down the road. Maisy glanced back at her friend. "It's surreal, you being here in this world."

"You're telling me! It's like something off the TV here."

Maisy laughed and dragged two of Ameera's bags over the road. "C'mon, I'll show you, my pad."

They trundled down the cobbled road, catching up. "It's so good talking to you in person again."

"You too. What have you been up to? How's Roxy?"

"Roxy's good, she's met some chef, so I've not seen much of her; has she been in contact with you?"

"The odd text, but I haven't spoken to her since I've been here."

"Well, nothing's changed really anyway."

Maisy led her over the field. "Man! My Converse feel soaked. Explains why you're wearing those ugly ass wellies."

"Sorry, yeah, you'll get filthy around here! I can't get around anywhere without these now." She opened the door. Ameera peered around her mouth open.

"Oh my god. I can't believe you've been living here. This place is so bad, man. And you! Of all people."

"It's not so bad, it's sort of cosy really. You should have seen it when I first arrived." She laughed, placing a piece of wood into the fireplace.

"I've got to admit, Maisy, so far, you've managed to shock me. And that's hard, man, you know I don't shock easily."

Ameera sat down at the kitchen table. Maisy carried Ameera's bags through to the bedroom.

"I'm so glad you're here! How tired are you from the journey?" she asked, settling the bags down on the floor.

"I'm okay."

"You must be hungry. I don't have that much in. Did you wanna go pub and get some dinner? I can introduce you to the locals."

"Yeah, man. Let me just take a shower and put a bit of make-up on then. Although I did already go in and meet the locals."

"You did? Shower's in here," she said, pointing into the bathroom.

"Yeah, your little man-thing's alright."

Maisy smirked. "Well I think so. Towels are in the cabinet by the toilet. And keep it casual. No one around here dresses up that much. I'll have to see if I can find you some boots at the farm."

Ameera made a sound, blowing air through her closed lips. "Forget that. My shoes are ruined anyway. I'll have to wear them for now. Can't believe these people couldn't even concrete a path for you."

"Well, it's only a temporary volunteer position. I don't suppose their funding is massive."

Ameera slipped into the bedroom and unzipped her suitcase.

"Is this the only bedroom?"

"Yeah, you can sleep in the bed. I'll go on the chair out here."

"Nah, don't be ridiculous. I can set up on the floor down here."

She pulled a small bodycon dress from her bag. Maisy looked at her. "Remember, low-key," she said, heading towards the kitchen.

"I'll try but I can't make myself any less good-looking. C'mon now." She smirked. "I've only got one razor with me. If we're here more than a couple of days, I'll need to pop shop."

"Oh, there's no popping to actual shops around here. But I should be able to make tomorrow my last shift. Then we can head back after if you like?"

Ameera walked from the bedroom; her arms piled in products. "Wait. No shops? How have you survived?"

"Well, there's one. They just don't have a lot. I usually make do or wait until someone goes into Inverness – although, speaking of which, I may need to go to a garden centre before I leave anyway."

"We can take my car if you want. I think I saw one on the A-road on the way here."

"Great. Shall we do that before we go pub? Not starving, are you?"

"I'll survive, I suppose. Where's your car anyway?"

"My maps sent me to a no-drive route. I had to leave it and walk down a twenty-odd-minute trail." Maisy could hear the tap turning on and off and Ameera banging and clunking the shower.

"You're jokes, man." Ameera laughed, her voice strained. "So, what you gonna do about the hunk?"

Had Ameera actually spoken to Davie? She wanted to ask her so many questions but didn't want to make a big deal out of it. Maisy walked into the bathroom behind her. "It's the taps! You just pull the little lever thingy up."

"What the..." She started tugging at the lever until it gave way with a clunk, the water burst through the shower with a hiss. Ameera stared at it open-mouthed and shook her head.

"So, did you speak to Davie?" Maisy asked, her stomach flipping.

"Yeah, I can see why you like him; I'll give you that. He's all dirty and manly, like a warrior. And you have always had a thing for alpha-male types when I come to think of it."

"No, I haven't."

"You so flipping have."

She started picturing her exes, they didn't look the same – but the last one was a boxer, the two before that had been business owners.

"What did he say, anyway?" she asked.

"Not a great deal, him and Craig and some old bloke were chatting shit mostly."

She heard the squeak of feet on the bathtub. "He didn't mention me?" she asked through the wall. But there was no response. Ameera was already in the shower. Maisy walked into the bedroom, a pain assaulting her stomach. Was he just carrying on as normal? Had he moved on without even speaking to her? Not seeing him felt like a physical pain somewhere deep inside – how could he just sit in the pub, like nothing was wrong? She felt like she was going to throw up. She wanted to get out of Illvenie as soon as possible; she needed to start her life all over again.

\*\*\*

It took them fifty-five minutes to find the garden centre Ameera had seen. It was almost 7pm by the time they got there. They found the plant just as the staff were closing.

"You're lucky. We stopped selling red maple in April. But we have one that has already grown to waist height. We can sell you that for half price, it just needs some tender love and care, it's a little wilted."

When they got back to the farmhouse, it was past eight. "Thank god for that, I'm starving."

"Ah about that."

"What now?" Ameera groaned.

"Well, they stop serving food at seven."

"Oh, c'mon, man. I'm knackered; I've been driving all day, waiting for you and you ain't even fed me."

"I promise I will find us some food; I just need to plant and water this before it gets any sicker. If all else fails, I do have pasta at the house."

"I'm surprised you even have an oven."

"Well, I do. It's small but I have one."

Reluctantly, Ameera followed her into the garden. Maisy dug a hole and planted the tree. Ameera moaned and whined as she helped dig the hole. She filled a watering can from the outside tap and wet the mud as Maisy buried it. The door creaked open, and Bob came strolling out, a crease between his eyes.

"What are you pair doing out here at this time of night?"

"Look!" she cried out, pointing to the tiny wilting tree amongst the now-beautiful garden. Ameera's upper lip lifted in confusion.

His eyes widened and he stepped closer. "Is it the one?" he asked, a look of enchantment on his face.

She nodded and grinned. "It is!"

He gasped. "I hope it lives through the winter."

"Me too."

"Well, I'll try my best to take care of it."

"I know you will," she said, smiling.

He turned to face her. "Thank you so much! I don't know what I'm going to do without you!"

"I don't know what I'll do without you either, Bob."

They stood for a moment, staring at the tree. Maisy's eyes wandered over the garden to Davie's house. The kitchen light was on, and she imagined him pottering around the kitchen in those flannel trousers that cupped his arse cheeks, cooking dinner or opening a beer, his wet hair hanging loose on his muscular shoulders.

"Who's your friend, Maisy?" Bob asked, shaking her from her thoughts.

"Sorry, Bob, this is Ameera. Ameera, Bob." They smiled at each other and nodded heads. "Actually, Bob, Ameera being here is one of the reasons I came to plant this tree tonight."

He turned to her, his eyes full of sadness. "You're going home?"

"I'm going home," she said solemnly. "Tomorrow, actually."

"Oh, Maisy." He sighed, his words like a punch to her stomach. They stood looking at the tree. She watched as Bob's eyes scanned the garden. He turned to her.

"Are you ladies in a rush? Angie made a huge casserole, none of us can manage it."

"Bob that sounds amazing, we missed dinner," she said, following him into the kitchen.

\*\*\*

Maisy was having a dream; she was kissing Davie, in the middle of a field, but her mum, dad and Miles were in the background calling her, complaining that she was doing it wrong.

"Maisy. Maisy. Maisy. Maisy," came a voice, hissing at her. She opened her eyes to find Ameera sitting next to her on the bed.

"What's wrong?"

"I think someone is outside."

Maisy sat up. "What?"

"Shhh. Maisy, there's a growling noise. It sounds like a weird bear or something."

Maisy flopped back into bed. "Oh, it's just the deer."

"That's not what a deer sound like."

Maisy grinned. "Honestly, it's just the deer. Go back to sleep."

"How can you sleep alone in this place? There are noises outside. I'm not lying, something is out there."

"It's just nature, Ameera."

"But the door doesn't lock. I don't like it."

"It's fine. Honest. I've survived it, haven't I?"

She could feel Ameera rocking by her side.

"Ameera. I promise you, it's fine."

"I'm sleeping in here with you then," she said, curling into Maisy's tiny bed. She felt her friend shaking. She turned over and closed her eyes. Maisy spun over and bunched up the quilt beneath her head. All was quiet.

"What was that?" Ameera whispered into the room.

"What? I didn't hear anything," she mumbled without opening her eyes.

"There was a bang."

"Probably the deer running away," she murmured.

"Fucking hell, man. Its' like living in the dark ages," she whispered. Her knee pressed into Maisy's back. Maisy rolled her eyes, then smiled to herself. She had actually forgotten about the noises. To her, they had melted into the background, like cars in the city or water trickling down a stream.

*What else might I be capable of?* she mused. *If I just saw things through, the way I've seen Corinuck through, I'd be capable of so much more.*

\*\*\*

When Maisy woke the next morning, Ameera was fast asleep, her arms stretched out across the bed. Maisy was hanging over the edge. Quietly, she rolled onto the floor and crawled towards the door.

She made coffee, then stood by the open front door. Her grey baggy pyjama bottoms were tucked into her woollen socks; the T-shirt tucked into the bottoms. It was warming up outside, the mist rising from the ground and rocks.

She placed her hand on her diaphragm and took some deep breaths in and out. She was going to miss the place; she felt at peace with herself for the first time in forever, she didn't want to go back to feeling like a lesser person. She looked up the hill in the direction of the farm, wondering what Davie was doing in that moment. She wanted to go to his house and declare her feelings for him, but he'd have been to see her if he felt the same way.

Ameera padded into the kitchen with a groan, her fringe flayed up and out. She was wearing jogging bottoms and a jumper on top of her pyjamas.

"Morning," Maisy said, raising her mug.

Ameera plonked herself down at the kitchen table with a huff. "Man, I don't know how you sleep in this place. It's basically a garden shed. What are you even doing here? There are no real men, no bars, no proper shops, the shower's clunky and the bed uncomfortable. It's a shit-hole, Maisy."

"It's rustic."

"Antiquated, you mean! Oh my god. Why have you got the door open?" she asked, hugging her knees into her chest and shivering. "It's bloody freezing, man."

Maisy nudged her head in the direction of the open door, the rolling misty hills and deer wandering around in the distance. Ameera got up and went to the door.

"What?"

"Jesus Christ, Ameera, how blind to the beauty of nature are you?"

Ameera raised her eyebrows. "The beauty of nature?" she scoffed. "Fucking hell, man."

Maisy looked out into the distance dreamily. "Some people see it as a better way of living. Out of the rat race."

"Pah. Those people are idiots."

Maisy rolled her eyes. "Coffee and pancakes?" she offered.

"I don't suppose you've got milk?"

"I have. Straight from Alfie's cows?"

"Ugh. You can get diseases from milk if it's not treated."

"Stop talking shit."

"I'm serious."

"You can get illnesses from too much saturated fat, alcohol, and preservatives too but that doesn't stop you does it. And it's all I've got. So, you'll like it or lump it."

"Fine," she said, rolling her eyes. "God, man, who are you and what have you done with Maisy?"

Maisy gave her a sarcastic smile back as she poured batter into the pan. "I've got to go and take care of Bob soon. Will you be okay for a couple of hours?"

"Hours? But it's so boring here," Ameera whined.

"Go for a walk."

"Ugh."

"The pub opens at eleven, if you get bored. I'll try and hurry up," she said, handing a plate of small pancakes over.

Ameera took them gratefully. She picked up the treacle syrup and squeezed it over the pancakes and took a slurp of coffee, banging it back down on to the table. "Fine, I'll go there. That Craig seems like an alright bloke anyway."

"Oh yeah?" Maisy said, eyeing her friend suggestively as she circled and tossed the pan.

"Oh, man! Don't be sick, I meant alright for a laugh. God, I ain't desperate, Maisy."

Maisy dropped pancakes on to another plate. "Don't be mean!" she sat on the chair, pancakes in hand. "And if you do go pub, don't drink, okay? We have a long drive home tonight."

"How can I go pub and not drink?"

"Drink lemonade."

"So, we're doing this then? Today?" Her eyes sparkled with excitement.

"I guess there's no time like the present," Maisy said with a sigh.

"You're not gonna change your mind later?" Ameera asked.

Her stomach tightened. "No, I'm ready. Let's get out of here."

Ameera stood up and started doing a dance, whooping. "Maisy's coming home, Maisy's coming home."

"I'll be ready. 5pm, okay?"

"5pm. Let's do it."

\*\*\*

When Maisy left the house, Ameera started packing back up what few bits she'd used. She got bored and decided to redraw her brows, add a little make-up, and change her clothes. At 12.15pm she walked up the hill. She could see the pub over the brow. A metallic blue BMW came screeching down Main Street – it was sleeker and newer than hers. This one had to be worth some money. It came to a stop outside of the farmhouse, where she'd been for dinner the previous night. The driver's door opened, and a short, stocky man wearing shades and joggers climbed out. He stealthily moved over to the passenger seat and opened it. A Jack Russell jumped out and ran toward the farmhouse gate. Ameera smiled to herself.

"Well, you're not from here are you now?" Ameera said.

He turned and looked at her, an amused smile playing on his lips.

Their eyes locked. He rubbed his face in joval disbelief.

"Are you a mirage?" he asked. "We don't get many beautiful women around here."

She grinned at him. "That the best you've got?"

He laughed. "Sorry, I'm pretty lame. Don't get enough practice round here. And if I'm honest, you've got me choked."

His Jack Russell stared at them and barked from the closed gate.

"Your dog escaped," she said.

"Oh, it's okay. He knows where he's going."

"You actually live in the farmhouse?" she asked in disbelief.

"God no." He laughed. She laughed with him. "No, I'd die if I had to live in Illvenie. My gran lives here – I come to visit." He widened his legs, putting his hands into his jogger pockets.

"That makes sense," she said on a laugh.

"I know you didn't really think I lived around these parts. I'm way too good-looking."

"You look normal, if that's what you mean."

He put both hands on his heart, pretended to be blown away. Ameera laughed.

Davie came walking down the hill and past them, he glanced over. "How's it going, Ameera?" he said stiffly.

She glanced at him briefly. "Hey, Davie."

He walked up the drive of the farmhouse, the Jack Russell following him inside.

"You've met Davie then?" BMW guy asked.

"Yeah, in the pub a couple of days ago."

"Boring twat," he said with a laugh. She gasped before giggling back.

"Boring place," she said in response. He raised an eyebrow.

"The name's Logan, by the way. What's yours?"

"Ameera."

"Ever been to Inverness, Ameera?"

# Twenty

Angie placed a glass of wine onto the table in front of Maisy. She didn't want to reject the drink, but she was going to be driving soon. She took a sip and decided that as soon as she could she was going to dispose of it.

Angie sat across to her. "Can you believe how many people have turned up to say goodbye?"

"Are you sure they're here for me?" Maisy asked.

"Yep, it's about half of the village! You must have made quite an impression, lass." She looked around. "Although us Scot's do like an excuse for a wee celebratory drink." She laughed.

"I'm still honoured." She said with a smile.

"And you should be!" Angie said, nudging her elbow into Maisy's ribs affectionately.

"D'ya know, this is the first place I've ever really felt wanted and comfy in my own skin." Her eyes filled with tears as she realised how honest her words were. Angie reached over and put her hand on top of Maisy's and dipped her head to watch Maisy's face. "Oh, my love. I wish I could offer you an actual job here. I just don't have the funding. And I don't imagine you can afford to work for free forever either, can you?"

Maisy smiled. "No, I know it's time to go home. I have to face real life again soon, eh?"

Angie smiled at her sympathetically. "What time are you heading off?"

"About 5pm. What time is it now?"

"Almost 3pm," she said, sticking out her bottom lip.

"Oh," Maisy replied, looking around the room. "I expected Ameera to be in here by now, have you seen her?"

"No, ask Craig, he might know."

She leant over the bar. Alfie was talking as Craig busied behind the bar, wiping glasses and stacking them away. "Well, I for one am glad the rain is clearing up. You ask Davie. The harvest has been slow this year. We went a whole fifteen days without crop ready to cut."

"It certainly has a massive impact," replied Craig. "One minute, Alfie. I think Maisy needs serving."

Alfie nodded then turned and gave Maisy a nod and a smile. Craig rotated his body towards her and leaned over the bar. "What can I get the guest of honour?" he asked.

"Sorry, I'm not after a drink, Craig. Did you see Ameera today, by any chance?"

"Nope, she hasn't been in. But you did miss Davie earlier."

Her stomach sank. "How is he?" she asked, her voice more subdued.

"Heartbroken," he said. They looked at each other. She inhaled deeply, and his face softened. "Pop in, Mais, say goodbye to him."

"Its best that I don't," she croaked.

"He said the same thing. Why are you both being so stubborn? I've never seen him like this with anyone."

"Well, if we're both saying the same, surely it means we're right."

He grimaced. "I'll keep my nose out. Look, it's been lovely getting to know you. I'm going to miss you around here, bringing life to this place. Take care of yourself, okay."

Suddenly, Craig dived over the bar and wrapped her in a huge hug. A tear rolled down her cheek. After that she was enveloped in hug after hug before making her way back to Corinuck.

As she walked down the hill. she noticed Ameera's car was still at the house. The nerves started bouncing around her stomach. "Here goes," she whispered to herself, opening the door to Corinuck.

The house was empty. She went into the bedroom; Ameera's bag was still sprawled out on the bed only half full. Her clothes laid over the bedroom floor. Where the hell was she?

\*\*\*

After pacing the house and allowing her thoughts to wander everywhere, frightening herself silly, Maisy ran up the hill to the farmhouse to ring Ameera. She jogged up behind the back gate and sat on the wall made of large salty rocks. As she did so her phone bleeped over and over, messages filtering through.

Mum: *Hey, how are you?*

Roxy: *How's the Highland life? Sorry I haven't been in*

*touch; you must be mad at me?? Has Ameera eaten all of the men alive yet? xxx*

Ameera: *Gone for drinks and food in Inverness, thought you might want time to say goodbye to your friends. Catch you later. X*

Maisy exhaled in relief. Inverness though! How random – she must have really been bored.

She clicked reply: *My god, Ameera!! I was worried about you. We're supposed to be leaving now. When will you be back?*

Her phone immediately pinged back.

Ameera: *No rush. Will let you know when on way.*

A sudden realisation dawned on her.

Maisy: *Wait, your car is here. Who have you gone with?*

She pressed send and waited for the ticks to turn green. With her phone in hand, and message open in front of her, Maisy stood up. She looked around the gate at Bob's beautiful garden and over to Davie's house. She stared at the light on the porch, switched on, swinging in the wind. Her eyes pixelated as memories flooded her mind. Davie dancing over her as he stripped off; the joy she'd felt as they ate together, woke up together, rode the horses together. Remembering the first date as she'd walked across the field. The way she'd felt when he had been there, on the deck, waiting for her. Her stomach whirled out of control. Davie was a one-off bloke. Not like anyone she'd ever met. He just seemed to get her. She hoped she meshed with someone else in the same way in the future. But she felt sad for him, imagining him all alone in his house.

Her phone pinged.

Ameera: *Some bloke whose grandma lives in the farm. Winky face xx*

"That fucking Logan." She said, exhaling loudly.

# Twenty-One

Davie had been considering his next move all day, like a game of chess he couldn't win. He so badly wanted to see Maisy before she left. But at the same time, he knew it would do neither of them any good, so he did nothing. Stalemate. He went to bed hoping the day would pass by and he could wake up and get back to his old life. But as he curled beneath his quilt in the darkness of his blackout blinds, his mind busied. What if his life never went back to what it was, and he remained unhappy forever, knowing what could have been? What if she did want him too but was waiting for him to say it first? What if he moved to Leicester to be with her, or they did the long-distant thing? What if she moved there? He would never know her thoughts because he hadn't even broached the subject with her. How could he? He barely knew her. *But it's Maisy*. A heat washed over him. What an idiot. Was he too late? He climbed out of bed, tied back his hair, chucked on his boots, laces loose, and drove his old flatbed down to the pub.

***

The place was heaving with locals. There were banners on the wall and balloons reading 'farewell'.

Davie gripped tight the small box in his pocket. *Was he ready for this? Was he really ready?* The girl had made an impression like no other.

He walked over to the bar, terrified of seeing her, but wanting to see her all at the same time.

"Davie," Craig called happily. "What can I get you, fella? Didn't expect to see you just yet."

"No, well, I want to catch her before she leaves."

Craig stared at him wide-eyed and gulped. "She's gone, my friend."

"Oh. She's already left?" he asked, sitting down, feeling the pub rock back and forth.

"About an hour ago."

"Probably for the best then, aye?" he said, his heading hanging low.

"She was asking after you," Craig said, pouring a pint for Davie.

"Aye, man," Davie replied, rubbing his chin, his stomach whirring out of control.

*I think I'm going to throw up.*

"I need to say goodbye. I can't let her go without…" He jumped off the stool and hurried out of the pub, hearing only the ringing of his ears and Craig hollering excitedly behind him. He jumped into his van and set the satnav to Leicester.

\*\*\*

Maisy sat on the kitchen chair with her suitcases, wondering what was taking Ameera so long. Neither of them really knew this Logan bloke; what if he wouldn't let her leave? She wouldn't be able to get to Inverness. She went into the bedroom and started sifting through Ameera's stuff, looking for her keys. She emptied the whole bag onto the bed, searched under it and all over it. They weren't there. *They must be with her in her bag.*

She packed up Ameera's belongings, folding them neatly, then she emptied the cupboards and fridge of anything perishable, leaving only a half bag of bread and a knob of butter. She walked the bags to the bin at the bottom of the road, drank several cups of black tea, and paced back and forth. At 9pm she ran up the hill in the dark; it was cooler out by then, but she was sweating. She opened the gate to the farmhouse and sat on the rock wall, waiting for the bleeps. Nothing came.

Maisy: *Ameera, this is taking the piss now. Where are you?*

It was opened. Ameera began typing then stopped. Maisy's breath hitched in her throat. She sent another text, typing frantically: *Ameera!!* She stood up on wobbly legs as a reply came through.

Ameera: *Chill, I told you I'll meet you at the house.*

Maisy: *We were supposed to leave at 5pm. I don't know this Logan bloke and neither do you. You shouldn't have gone with him.*

Ameera. *I'm fine. Leaving soon.*

*Leaving soon! Leaving soon?* It was already 9.27pm – that meant she wouldn't be back until after eleven. They couldn't drive overnight, could they?

She stepped up on the stile behind her and looked out at Davie's house. It was in complete darkness, his van gone. *Where are you, Davie?* Slowly, Maisy strolled back to Corinuck, kicking at the gravel, a heavy feeling in the pit of her stomach.

\*\*\*

With three quick coffee and wee breaks, and a fuel fill-up, it took Davie near on eleven hours to get to Leicester. As he approached the city, his van started making a loud thumping noise; he could smell burning. The smell getting stronger with each mile.

Leicester roads had a handful of cars travelling along both sides, despite it being only 4am. He hadn't expected to see anyone. The roads were also filled with parked cars. He had arrived. *Okay, so what now? I hadn't thought past getting here.*

He didn't even know how he was going to find her. All he knew was that she drank in a place called R-bar and her father owned a business called Fowler's Homes.

He pulled over and typed 'Fowler's Homes' into his phone. It came straight up; the main office was situated in a place called Narborough Road. He drove along, past buildings in a row, one after another. The only light came from a massive Tesco supermarket and a few passing headlights. He spotted Fowler's; the sign was lit up. He found a space down the road and sat in his van for a few minutes. He'd driven over ten hours to possibly be rejected. But he remembered the story Bob had told him, about Carey and her indecisiveness, how he'd fought for her because he'd rather have been rejected by Carey than chased by anybody else.

He hunched down in his seat and took a catnap.

# Twenty-Two

Robert Fowler was a short, chubby man with a bald head. He was dressed in a smart shirt, open at the collar and grey pipe-lined baggy trousers. His round face was friendly but serious, like he meant business, despite the fact that Davie towered over him as he wiggled the huge set of keys in an attempt to open the double doors. His demeanour reminded Davie of Alfie in some ways. But he could see where Maisy's bright green eyes came from.

"We don't normally have people waiting by our door at 6.30am." He laughed. "Our sales team don't actually get in until nine." He spoke as he walked around switching on lights and opening blinds in the large open office space. Davie stood and stared; words seemed to have evaded him.

Robert stopped what he was doing and looked back at Davie like he was a little slow. "How can I help you, mate?" he asked slowly.

"Aye, sorry, erm." He coughed. "I shouldnee come, fella. I don't know why I'm here. I'll just go." He turned.

"Wait. You're Scottish?"

Davie turned around. "Aye."

He narrowed his eyes. "Live around here?" he asked, eyebrows raised.

Davie shook his head. "So, you've driven here from Scotland?"

Davie nodded in response.

The man's eyes furrowed, his shoulders droop and he inhaled a sharp breath. "What did she do?" he asked. His lips pressed in a straight thin line. Davie looked back at him, feeling his own eyes widen in surprise. "It's okay, you can tell me. I'm not one of those parents who thinks their kid is always right."

Davie was a little annoyed by the comment. He understood what Robert meant, those parents whose kids misbehaved and they claimed their Jonny would never bully or torment other kids. But he was assuming that she'd done something, that she was in the wrong and his first question hadn't been of concern for his daughter's welfare but an assumption that she was guilty of something. He obviously didn't know the Maisy Davie knew. Not a kid, but a woman. A woman he knew was strong-willed, smart, caring, beautiful, funny, quirky, and sweet. A woman who was also massively insecure. Was this why? Had her parents always expected the worse from her? Never battled for her honour. Well, he would.

Bob wasn't even his biological father and yet if anyone had accused Davie of anything, he'd always assumed Davie had a good reason for his actions. Bob and Carey's blind faith had made him want to do better. Bob had also been the one who had accused him of being in love with Maisy. *Is he in love with her? Is that why he is here?*

Oh shit! Who drove five hundred miles to tell someone goodbye? 'A man in love,' said Bob's voice in his head.

"Come on, what's she done?" Robert repeated. He was switching on his computer then. Shuffling through paperwork, watching Davie with interest.

"You didn't ask if she's okay," he said.

"I don't need to; she's like a Spanish bull that girl," he said with a fond smile. Okay so he did love her. He just had an ill-judged opinion of her. Maybe it was an old version of the woman he'd fallen in love with, but it wasn't her now, it wasn't the real Maisy.

"I don't want to be rude, but my staff are going to start coming in in a couple of hours. And I don't fancy them knowing all my personal business. How can I help you, fella?"

"I just want to know if I can see her. I need to speak to her."

Robert paused, holding a paperclip on the top of a pile of papers. "Then why are you here? As far as I know, she's in Scotland."

"She left last night. An hour or so before me."

"Oh. Maybe she arrived since I left the house. Sorry, what was your name again?"

"Davie Marshall."

Robert picked up his phone and put it to his ear. "Kathy!" he called into the speaker. "Maisy home?" He stood quietly for a moment, listening. "She mentioned a Davie to you?" he nodded along. "He's here."

Davie heard a squeak from the phone. Robert smiled then turned his back to Davie, perching on the edge of his desk as he nodded his head. He hung up just as a woman walked into the office. She was petite, middle-aged, and dressed in a pinny. She carried a bucket of cleaning products through.

"Morning, Rob," she yelled as she bounded past him.

"Morning," he called back. He turned to Davie. "So, the last Kathy heard – Maisy was still waiting for Ameera to arrive back. Said she'd gone to a party without her or something."

He remembered Ameera talking to Logan outside the farmhouse. He exhaled a breath he'd been holding, unaware. "She's still in Scotland?" he asked.

"As far as I know. You better take a seat. I'll get the kettle on."

"No, it's fine. If Ameera is with who I think she's with, they might not even come back today. I'll go home."

"Mate, you've just driven god-knows how many miles; you can't do it again on no sleep."

"I took a little catnap in the car. If I need another I will stop."

"At least let me get you some coffee to take with you."

"Okay. Thank you."

# Twenty-Three

Maisy was woken by a loud bang. She jumped up from the kitchen table, wiped a string of dribble from her mouth and stretched out her aching neck. Ameera was walking through the door, looking a little crumpled. She was also still dressed in the previous night's clothes. Maisy turned to the window; it was starting to get light outside. A loud engine revved away. Ameera smiled awkwardly.

"Morning," she said.

"What time is it?" Maisy mumbled, rubbing at her face.

"Just gone 6am."

Maisy screwed up her face. "Where in god's name have you been?"

"I texted you. I went on a night out in Inverness."

"With Logan?"

"Oh my god, you know him?!" She laughed, sitting on the chair by Maisy. She put her head into her hands.

"Of course I know him, I went on a date with him when I first got here."

"Oh, you know him like I know him?"

"No, I didn't stop out with him. He's a player."

"Players' gotta play."

"What does that even mean?" Maisy replied, dry scrubbing her cheeks irritably.

"It is what it is. Why are you getting so emotional for? You've got Davie. God, you can't have them all to yourself."

Maisy felt the irritation itching at her feet. "It's not about that. Ameera, I was ready to leave, I left the pub early to meet you. You let me down and I was worried sick that something bad had happened to you."

"Ugh. I've got a hangover, stop being so loud, man."

"You've got a hangover? I've just slept slumped over this uncomfortable table all night, worrying in case you'd been abducted."

"I don't see any police." She laughed.

"Because my subconscious knows what you're like. But what if I was wrong?"

"Anyways, that table, can't be much worse than the bed here. Fucking hell, man, if I wanted a night out with Roxy, I'd have just gone out with *her*."

Maisy sat up, appalled, and stared at her friend. "It's called consideration, you ought to give it a try."

"Alright, fine. Just stop whining, please. You're not my wife for god's sake."

Maisy looked up, furrowing her brow at her friend.

"You've changed, man. What have you done with my fun friend? The one who used to go missing *with* me."

Maisy stood up and flicked on the kettle. "Maybe I've grown up. Maybe it's time you did too."

"Ugh," she moaned, flopping her head deeper into her arms. Maisy made Ameera a black coffee. She sat up straight and took it from her gratefully. "Sorry, man. I honestly believed that you weren't gonna come back home with me last night."

"Why?"

"Because it's obvious you've got the feels for this Davie bloke. And I've never known you to settle with unclosed business."

She took a sip of coffee. Maisy shook her head. "Let's just leave. You okay to drive me to my car?"

"We got any food first? I'd better eat – I was proper wasted last night, you know."

Maisy sighed and got up to open the cupboard. "There's a couple of pieces of bread left. Want toast?"

"That'll have to do till we get to the services."

Maisy dropped the last two pieces of bread into the toaster and pushed down the lever, then topped up their cups with more coffee.

"Maisy, don't be pissed at me please. I've been having a hard time and you ain't been around. I've barely even heard from you."

Maisy turned around, leaning on the counter. "I know, I'm sorry, you're right. You're always there for me and I've let you down since I've been here. Want to talk about it? Are your family stressing you out?"

Ameera yawned and rubbed at the mascara from under her eyes. "They'd stopped hassling me for a while and I thought maybe they'd given up. Turns out they've been going behind my back arranging a wedding for me. I've never even met this guy, man, what am I supposed to do?"

"Oh, you're kidding! I didn't know your family did that! They didn't do it for your sisters did they?"

"No but those guys were married by twenty-five. Actually, by twenty. And here I am, near on twenty-six with no prospects even on the horizon."

"So, what are you going to do?"

"Maybe I'll move out here with you." She laughed. The toast popped up; Maisy pulled her eyebrows down at Ameera before turning to grab the toast.

"I ain't marrying no stranger. I'd rather marry you."

"Well, I wouldn't marry you. You're a pain in the arse."

"Says the one."

\*\*\*

Maisy sat in Ameera's BMW, glad to be back in her ballet pumps, cosy jumper, and leggings. Ameera had showered and put on tracksuit bottoms and a jumper. She was looking casual and fresh, she smelt of aloe vera and rosehip body wash. Spotify linked up to the car and started playing rap.

"Can I change this music?" asked Maisy, picking up the phone.

"Fucking hell, man, I don't get in your car and change your tunes, do I?"

"That's because I don't listen to shite. I mean Dave! What's actually wrong with you?" They laughed at each other.

Maisy put Stoney on and dropped the phone back into the drink holder.

"Can't believe how long you took to get ready. It's almost 11am!"

"You're like a nagging wife! We will be home before bedtime, innit, what you worried about?"

*Home.* Her stomach ached. Where was home? She remembered first meeting Davie; he'd looked at her like she was an alien. She remembered calling him a hillbilly, how he'd grinned at her like she was a puppy. She imagined being home, back in Leicester. In a house where everything was so much easier but didn't bring her joy.

What was she going back to? Why was she going back? What if she never felt this way about anyone ever again? She hadn't felt like a failure in Scotland, she'd felt accepted, wanted, even. Who would Bob talk to now? The thoughts spinning through her mind made her feel sick. She couldn't breathe, felt something pressing down on her throat, felt the spaced-out blur in her eyes she hadn't felt for months. She should have stayed and given them a fighting chance. What if it was meant to be? She put a hand on her diaphragm, breathed deep. *Illvee-yakee.* She wiggled her toes, concentrating on the feelings of her feet, picturing the view from Bob's garden and the feel of Davie beside her. She felt a calm envelope over her. *Illvee-yakee.*

"I think it was just what I needed. Going there," she murmured.

"Maybe. You do seem much more settled in yourself, you know," said Ameera.

"Yeah, it's not my Family's fault that I'm not happy at home. I had some problems knowing myself. I was angry and I treated them badly. Then I was stuck in a cycle because they only knew me that way – how could I escape the person I was to them?"

"Bloody hell, man, I thought you were gonna go back and rub it in their faces. You did it, man. You proved them wrong."

"I ain't bothered about that. It's not what's important in the grand scheme of things."

"Do you think things will be different now?"

"I don't know. Nothings actually changed, has it? Maybe we are just bad for each other. Maybe we will fall back into our old ways. I should have stayed a bit longer or found a job elsewhere whilst I was there."

"You sound like you're freaking out about going back…"

"I am," Maisy said on a laugh.

"Yeah, but you lived with them for twenty-five years. I'm sure they missed you. Look, once you get home, find a new job – something a bit more suited to you, I'm sure you'll feel differently. I still think you can take this little life lesson with you."

"I suppose." She sighed. But she wasn't ready to go back. She had still wanted to explore the possibility of her and Davie, it was only just starting really.

They turned onto the thin mountain road. "Is it this one?"

"Yeah."

Her car groaned and creaked over the rough road. "I can't believe you followed the maps up here, man, I'd have shit myself."

"I didn't have much choice, it said this was the way. Just follow it up the hill."

The road was getting tighter. "Fucking hell man. Am I gonna be able to turn around up here?"

"Yeah, there's a turning point where I'm parked."

They pulled up at the side of Maisy's car. She opened the car door and grabbed her bags.

"Meet you at the services once we're on the M6?"

Ameera turned off the engine. "Maisy, see if your car works first. It's been sat here for months."

She approached her car, pressing the unlock button. Nothing happened.

"There should be a key inside your key fob. I'll get the jump leads."

Maisy pulled the key from the fob. "How did you know that?"

Ameera shrugged. Maisy got in and attempted to start the engine. It made a tiny noise, like a coin dropping.

"It is dead. Maybe it's a sign?"

Ameera walked back towards the car. "A sign that you left your car without starting the engine for months. What did you expect, man?"

"Still can't believe you have jump leads, Mrs fly-by-the-seat-of-my-pants."

"Doesn't mean I'm not organised, just cus I'm spontaneous." She sniggered, opening the bonnet.

Maisy watched her clip the jump leads on. "Ameera? Why don't you go on a date with this guy your parents have lined up. See what he's like? I know your parents; if he's no good, they ain't going to make you marry him."

Ameera twiddled her fingers. "I know that – I just hate the idea of it. But maybe I could give him a try. I mean, if Logan is the dating pool, it can't get much worse, can it?" She laughed.

"I knew you didn't like him!" Maisy scoffed.

Ameera got into her car and started up the engine. Maisy looked down at her shoes; the mud stains hadn't completely gone – she could still see them, but she didn't care. She smiled to herself, gulping down the lump in her throat. She loved her friend; Ameera was always there for her, she could always cheer her up when she was feeling down. And though she usually caused the trouble, she'd never leave Maisy's side. If she left, she'd miss her like crazy. But things were changing, it was inevitable.

With Davie, she felt capable of doing things for herself, she hadn't felt the need to take risks, drink too much or smoke. Leaving him was breaking her heart in two.

*I don't want to go home* chanted through Maisy's mind like a freight train. She didn't want to be the old Maisy ever again.

Ameera stood next to her, staring at her phone.

"I mean, the guy ain't bad looking."

She flashed a photo to Maisy; the man was tall with a beard and kind eyes.

"It wouldn't hurt to go on a date, I suppose."

Maisy turned to her friend. "What have you got to lose?"

"Exactly."

Maisy stared at the road over the brow of the hill they were standing on.

"You okay?"

"I was just thinking. We've been friends for a long time."

"We have. And here I am again, saving your ass."

"Yes, and I love you, but…"

Ameera stood up, blew her fringe off her forehead, and stared back at her friend, a knowing look on her face.

"Start the car and get out of here. You know you want to go back and find him."

"I can't just go…"

"For what it's worth, I think you're being a dickface. But you're gonna do what you're gonna do, innit."

"Dickface?"

Ameera giggled. Maisy sat in the driver's seat and turned the key in the ignition. On the second attempt, the engine roared to life. Ameera unclipped the jump leads. Maisy got out and wrapped herself around her friend.

"I swear to god, man!" Ameera complained as she wiped a tear from her face with the back of her hand. Maisy looked her in the eye. "You're fucking annoying," Ameera said.

"I know." Maisy sighed. "Meet you back home tomorrow?"

"If you come back!" she exclaimed, wrapping the jump leads around her hand.

"I could be back tonight if he tells me to buggar off."

"No man's gonna ever tell you to buggar off, Maisy. Let's be realistic here."

"If not, I'll be back for your wedding."

"Fucking hell, more likely to be yours than mine."

"Pah!"

Maisy drove away, butterflies ambushing her stomach as Ameera pulled off into the opposite direction.

# Twenty-Four

Maisy drove straight to the farmhouse. She texted her mum with an update. She paced back and forth on Bob's drive, practising what she would say to Davie. *Illvee-Yakee.* She grinned before jogging across the field, laughing as she dodged cowpats, mud squishing inside her ballet flats. She stepped up onto his porch and knocked hard on the door three times. There was no reply. She continued to knock, but no one came. Notifications bleeped on her phone... it had automatically reconnected to his Wi-Fi. Maybe she should WhatsApp call him.

She tried the door handle. It opened. "Davie?" she sang into the quiet. No one came. She shut it and trapsed back over the field. She went to Alfie's farm. Alfie was driving around the other side of the field on a combined harvester; he was alone. She looked at her watch. It was 1.30pm. She walked down the drive and to the pub, opening the heavy door with a swing.

Craig was inside with his back to her; he was talking to a delivery driver. A woman she'd seen once or twice was serving. "Can I get you anything?"

Maisy hesitated. "Just a coffee, thanks." Her eye was on Craig.

"You sure?" the woman asked.

"Huh?" Maisy asked, turning back to look at her.

"Have you tasted the coffee here? It's like shit water."

Maisy laughed. Honesty was the Illvenie way. "I'll drink anything," she replied with a grin. Craig turned and caught her eye, then did a double take.

"Maisy!" he yelled. "What in the… Oh my god! Did Davie actually bring you back? Where is he?"

"Bring me back from where? That's what I came to ask you? What?"

"What yourself. Davie went to Leicester. He went to see you, wanted to say goodbye properly or something!"

"Oh my god!" she screeched and ran from the pub.

"What about your coffee?" The woman's call died out and she shrugged.

Craig turned to her. "Why's everyone keep running out on me?" As Maisy flew out of the double doors, she heard Craig calling after her, "Maisy, wait," but she had no time to waste. She had to get back to Leicester. Davie was looking for her. Davie had driven to Leicester to find her.

\*\*\*

As she passed Glasgow on the motorway, Maisy realised that her petrol gauge was under the red line. "Shit!" She gasped. She took the next turning off the A9, looking for a petrol station. There were none in sight. She pulled up and searched her satnav. BP was one mile to the east. She drove up a hill, begging her car to keep moving. The fuel station was in sight, she was twitching to get there. "C'mon, c'mon," she mumbled at the car, as the traffic lights turned red. On the opposite side, it looked as though a flatbed had broken down at the side of the road; it was a bit like Davie's and brought back memories of her second day in Illvenie when he'd brought back all the bric-a-brac furniture he'd collected from locals. Initially, she'd been horrified, but once it was all in and cleaned up, she'd felt a creative side she never knew she had, painting and polishing and putting it all together. Her and Davie had made the little place look so homey, and they'd had a laugh doing it.

The lights turned green and she nudged forward with the flow of traffic. She peered around behind the open bonnet; a man stood tall. He had long hair and wide shoulders; a Viking look to him. It couldn't be, could it? She opened her mouth as her car slid by. He glanced up, caught her eye and jumped. Bumping his head on the open bonnet. She braked and moved to the right lane, a car behind papping at her aggressively. *Too close.* She knew. The opposite side of the road was empty – swiftly, she turned the car around pulling her steering wheel all of the way. Tears filling her eyes, she stepped out onto the gravelled road. She hesitantly opened the door. Before she knew it, he was pulling her from her car, his arms wrapped around her waist; she was pressed into his hard chest feeling like she was home.

She cried into his neck. "I didn't think I'd see you again."

"I couldnee go forever without you."

For a long moment they stood, leaning against her car, their bodies so close they could be one, their breaths heavy against one another.

"You broke down?" she asked into his neck.

"Yes. I think the old fellas had his day." He leaned back and looked at her, his eyes wandering over her face.

She smiled at him solemnly. Cars were zooming by, shaking her car, rocking them.

"What are you doing around here, anyway? You're miles out," Davie said. "And where's your pal?"

"Oh, she's driving back to Leicester. I turned around to come back and realised I was out of diesel."

"You just left Illvenie?" he asked, smirking.

"Yes."

He sniggered to himself, putting his head into her hair.

"When did you leave, anyway?" Maisy asked.

"Last night! I've already been to Leicester. I even met your dad." He scoffed.

"What? You're kidding?" She gulped, pulling back and staring into his eyes.

"Nope. I left after you left the pub last night. I thought you were going home."

"I was but there was this whole thing with Ameera, and we ended up leaving this morning instead."

"I know. She was with Logan the... hang on a minute. Maisy? Why were you going back to Illvenie?"

She rolled her eyes. "I think you know why."

"What a pair, hey?" She shivered. "Come on. Let's get you home. I can get the truck later."

She opened the door back up. "Corinuck is not my home anymore."

"No but Illvenie is, eh?" He raised his eyebrows suggestively and she grinned. Davie ran off and locked up his truck before climbing into her passenger seat. She started up the engine.

"We could have ridden the motorway for days, the rate we were going."

"I know! I stupidly didn't ask Craig when exactly you left."

"You could have just called."

"I know. You could have called me too if you thought I'd left."

"I wanted to say goodbye in person."

She turned to him. "You were really coming to say goodbye?"

"That was just an excuse."

"Thank god." She sighed, pulling back onto the road.

"I just need to go petrol station."

"I actually just came to tell you something."

"Oh?" she asked, dread filling her chest.

"Yeah, I hear Alfie's looking for a new vet."

She grinned. "I'm not a vet, Davie. I need to qualify."

"I'm sure he will wait. What's six years between friends, eh?"

Maisy laughed.

When she pulled up at the petrol station she didn't want to get out, didn't want to walk away from him. She filled up and paid as quickly as she could, as she walked back over the forecourt, she looked at him sat in her passenger seat. Butterflies filled her stomach and she grinned from the inside out.

She tugged on her seatbelt and started up the engine, they smiled at each other.

"Mais, I need you to know, when you said goodbye

to everyone last night, it took me less than ten minutes without you to realise that I need you."

She turned to face him. "You do?" she asked.

"I should have fought for you from the start. Then you'd have known you were wanted and needed. I was so scared of rejection that I didn't show you how I felt. I'm an idiot. You deserve a man who will fight for you, Maisy. I'm sorry. I hate the idea of losing you."

"You can't lose me, Davie. I'm pretty certain I'm in love with you." There. She'd said it. It felt so much more real said out loud; her insides were clattering.

"I love you too," he said, and she grinned. She swallowed; her throat was short of saliva. A tear spilt down his cheek. She leaned over and wiped it away then she kissed the damp skin.

"Take me home," she whispered.

"Gladly. Although you're in the driver's seat, baby."

"I am, aren't I?" She grinned. Turning away and pulling off the hand break, she waited for another car to pull off and she followed them to the exit.

"What will you do about the van?" she asked.

"I'll get Alfie's tow truck later."

"Imagine if we'd both broken down in the same place?" she mused aloud, re-entering the roundabout.

"I'd call that fate," she glanced at him, smiling thoughtfully. That was when she spotted it, the small navy-blue box gripped in his hands. All of a sudden, the seat belt felt as though it was restricting her chest.

# Epilogue

"The ceremony was beautiful, you looked gorgeous walking down the aisle." Davie mused, bending to wrap his arms around Maisy's waist and pull her in. She turned, laughing and looked up into his eyes. "I'm not marrying you yet Davie. I've already told you this."

"I know, it was worth a try. Wanna dance?"

"Nah. I'm just enjoying watching at the minute."

Maisy leaned her head against him. She was dressed in a pink-and-gold meshed *sari*, with dangly earrings, gold eyeshadow, and her hair was tied in a bouffant on top of her head. She watched out over the dance floor. The room was an array of colourful *saris*, *sherwanis* and *lehengas*, the walls and ceilings decorated in silks and bright, loose fabrics. She watched as they danced.

"I'm going to be dragged out soon." She could feel butterflies whirling in her stomach.

"Ah, the reason you had to come back so early. The dance wars."

She laughed. "It feels like I've been training for a flash mob."

"Then I can't wait to see it."

She inhaled deeply. "They look so happy," she said, grinning. "Don't they look so happy?"

Davie nodded. "I never expected Ameera to settle down. That one was a flipping wild card."

"I know, now look at her. They're even talking about having babies."

"You know you could be that happy too, if you'd accept my proposal."

She glanced up at him, grinning. He looked so handsome in his suit, his hair tied back and beard trimmed. "Let it go. I'm already that happy, just the way things are."

"I know, I know." He sighed.

Maisy's parents approached; her mum was in a baby-blue trousered suit with kitten heels. Maisy took the glass of wine from her mum's hands. Her dad put his arm around her waist and she rested her head on his shoulder. Her dad leaned in. "They're serving alcohol!" he whispered, taking a sip of his Jack Daniel's.

Maisy looked up at him. "C'mon, Dad, it's Ameera. Like she's not going to have alcohol at her wedding."

He smiled. "She's not the Ameera I remember."

"She's certainly done some growing up lately."

"Do you think you two will get married?" he asked, nodding towards Davie.

"I've heard enough. Did he ask you to say that?"

"No, I'm just curious."

"Well, then I'll answer once. I'm busy with the surgery and studies right now, I just want to concentrate on that."

He kissed her head. "Good girl. So, when are you both heading back to Scotland?"

"Sunday afternoon, I'm afraid. I have a diabetic cat and a bluetongue cow to get back to."

"Ahh." Robert nodded and winked at his wife. Maisy gave him a smirk. "Free for Sunday brunch before you leave?" he asked.

"Of course," replied Maisy. "Sam already invited me though. She said Miles is making a full English."

"Great..."

A row of women in matching dresses all held hands. They ran over and grabbed Maisy, pulling her onto the dance floor. They began the moves she'd been practising all week. Together, they raised the roof, skimmed the floor, and twisted their hands in the air.

A crowd developed around them and gradually people started to join in. First children, then elders and family members of the bride and groom, until eventually the floor was full. Maisy watched Ameera spinning around, hair flailing, grinning happily. She'd never seen her friend look so rosy-cheeked radiant. She wrapped her arms around Ameera's neck.

"Congratulations! Wow, Ameera, you have a serious glow on. It makes me so happy."

Maisy looked over at Davie. He was bopping his head to the music. She grinned. *What a goof.* He hadn't seen her, and so, for a while, she watched him as he smiled and spoke to people passing by.

"Who knew an assisted marriage was the way to go for me. Maybe I did have some good karma after all. I thought I'd cursed it all away," she said, laughing. "I must have done something right."

As Maisy turned to look back at Davie, she realised

he was watching her. The room was busy with dancing and excited chatter, the music was loud, but as their eyes connected; their bodies appeared to exhale in unison.

"Yeah." She sighed. "I know what you mean."

This book is printed on paper from sustainable sources managed under the Forest Stewardship Council (FSC) scheme.

It has been printed in the UK to reduce transportation miles and their impact upon the environment.

For every new title that Troubador publishes, we plant a tree to offset $CO_2$, partnering with the More Trees scheme.

For more about how Troubador offsets its environmental impact, see www.troubador.co.uk/sustainability-and-community